REVIEWS FOR *TYLER'S HILL*

Tyler's Hill captures the wonderment, hope, fear, excitement, and magic of that time in all our lives when the transition from the world of our childhood requires questioning and examination. The author has captured the essence of that transition. *Tyler's Hill* reminds us of our own transition no matter how complicated it may have been, and thus makes the story familiar to us. It is also a story of hope and excitement and the life that lies ahead for each of the characters. Through the characters, the author, in a unique way, addresses real life problems, and guides us through those experiences, leaving us with some, but not all, of the answers. This is a story for all ages; if you are twelve years old like *Tyler's Hill's* characters, Sandy, Lynn, Beth, and Mary, you will readily identify with them. If you are older, *Tyler's Hill* will reinvigorate the child in you.

      Dr. Richard White, Research Scientist and Psychologist

Tyler's Hill is a magical coming-of-age story that draws the reader into the joys and challenges facing twelve-year-old Sandy Lowenthal as change comes to her neighborhood.

Set in 1966, this is a story of how Sandy and her friends navigate through sixth grade. It follows the friends through the joys of newfound friendship and adventure, the terrible loss of a parent, and the struggle to accept and love those as different. Joined together in a "mystery," this delightful team of friends teaches us all to embrace and delight in our differences of culture and faith. A must read for parents and young adults who see the world as our neighborhood.

      Linda Whittaker, Psychotherapist and Creativity Coach

Tyler's Hill allows a leisured glimpse into that middle time of childhood when the longing for self-determination collides with the constraints imposed by the adult world that makes the rules. Filled with vivid scenes that convey a dauntless belief in possibilities, this book is rich with everything young readers love: adventure, struggle, hope—even a haunted house!

But Susan Katz mines even more deeply, addressing, with daring and depth, the religious and cultural elements that attend all the joys, fears, and desires of a group of girls coming of age together, learning about loss and the meaning of friendship. The adventures of twelve-year-old Sandy Lowenthal and her friends are as alluring and relatable to the modern young reader as Tom's, Becky's, and Huck's were a century ago.

Bernadette McBride, Adjunct English Professor,
Temple University

Tyler's Hill

Susan B. Katz

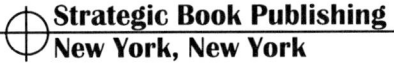
Strategic Book Publishing
New York, New York

Copyright © 2009

All rights reserved – Susan B. Katz

No part of this book may be reproduced or transmitted in any form or by any means, graphic, electronic, or mechanical, including photocopying, recording, taping, or by any information storage retrieval system, without the permission, in writing, from the publisher.

Strategic Book Publishing
An imprint of Writers Literary & Publishing Services, Inc.
845 Third Avenue, 6th Floor – 6016
New York, NY 10022
http://www.strategicbookpublishing.com

ISBN: 978-1-60860-172-1

Printed in the United States of America

Book Design: Suzanne Kelly

Dedication

Dedicated to mothers and their daughters

In memory of Bernard Katz, Helen and Erwin Ernst.

Inspired by true events.

Acknowledgements

Exhausted from the recent move from Chicago to Philadelphia, my husband said to me, "Susan, can you please go back to the storage bin and see if the movers got everything?" So, I did. The initial inspection proved that, indeed, the movers had done their job. The storage bin stood bare. I was about to return to supervise the movers' placement of our household items in our new home. However, something beckoned me to the corner of the storage bin where a small piece of paper laid on the ground. I picked it up and through the smudges I read the premise for *Tyler's Hill* that I wrote a year earlier. It was an ah-ha moment letting me know that I must write this novel. Of course, with small children to care for and trying to build a new life in a new community the question was, when would I have the time?

This segues into a full acknowledgement and appreciation for my husband, Dr. Richard White, for everything he is in my life – and for sending me back to check the storage bin. Without that experience, this book would never have been written. Richard has been my strongest supporter for the creative writer that exists inside me. I admire his strength, courage, love, and devotion to our family and me. I love him deeply.

This year marks my mother's ninety-first birthday. She, too, has been a strong supporter of my creative endeavors. When the world premiere of my first play, "Courage Untold," played in Chicago she flew in from Detroit to see the performance. She never missed any of my stage performances when I was a young girl and young adult. She was, indeed, the proud mom, always sitting in the first row, and nodding her head in approval. It was from my mother that I learned self-confidence, and that I could do anything I put my mind to. Thank you, Mom, for being my mother. Your unconditional love has been a transformational force in my life.

Lastly, I wish to thank my sister, Dr. Linda Katz, who is the greatest sister on the planet. There is no one I know who gives more fully from her heart than her. She is the only one who is allowed to see my first draft of a creative work, and the only one who can let you know that this is a "do-over" without hurting your feelings. I love you, my sister, and thank you for your endless support.

Tyler's Hill

CHAPTER 1

Bulldozers

Puddles of sticky motor oil covered the ground. The jarring blast of an engine startled the blackbirds. Hundreds screamed into the sky. Feathers scattered. They burst above the trees and flew from Tyler's Hill.

It was the summer of 1966 in a typical middle-class, white, suburban neighborhood of Detroit. All the houses looked the same—small, three-bedroom, brick ranch houses, each with a small rectangular lawn in front and a small rectangular back yard, where the children often played. All the sprinklers were operating on this hot, humid, Monday morning—everyone trying to keep the grass from browning. The sun, although still positioned low on the powder-blue horizon, was already emitting strong heat at 8:00 a.m.—today promised to be a Midwest scorcher.

In one of the houses on Lincoln Street lived an eleven-year-old, freckled-face girl named Sandy. She had brown, shoulder-length hair, parted down the middle, and bangs that edged near to the top of her eyebrows. She wore stylish tortoise-shell glasses that highlighted her green eyes. She rushed to put on her shoes and ran out the door with a glass jar in her hand. When she was halfway down the block, her mother yelled, "Sandy, where are you going in such a hurry?"

Sandy tried to avoid the sprinkler systems, and yelled back, "Tyler's Hill!"

Sandy often planned her days to sit thinking at Tyler's Hill. She had an active imagination. The spot was named Tyler's Hill because it was located three football fields behind Tyler Elementary, where Sandy and her friends attended school.

This was Sandy's last year in elementary school. In the fall, she'd enter the sixth grade. Tyler Elementary was the only school she had ever known. She liked it there and was popular, but now only four weeks out on summer break, Sandy was getting bored. Sitting at Tyler's Hill, she thought, *Maybe I shoulda gone to camp, too. Lisa, Patty, Lynn, and Carol are going. Well, it's too late now.* She slumped to her side. Within minutes, a loud sound jolted her upright.

She peered down the flat Midwestern landscape from high on her hilltop and saw and heard the bulldozers at work, destroying the woods and open fields next to Tyler's Hill. She pulled her knees up to her chest and grabbed her arms around them and whispered, "They're crushing my wild strawberry fields. This means my pond is next." She pressed her face hard into her knees, shielding her eyes from the massacre.

When Sandy asked her dad last month if he could stop the bulldozers from destroying the fields and woods, he shook his head. "I'm sorry, dear. Mr. Potter sold that land to a developer who will be building a new subdivision. You could have many new friends this year."

Sandy stomped her foot. "Dad, I don't need any more friends! I don't need these stupid new houses. We need the woods. Where else can me and my friends catch tadpoles?"

It was for this reason that Sandy brought her glass jar to Tyler's Hill. Today, she planned to go to her favorite pond and catch tadpoles for the last time before the bulldozers and lumberjacks demolished it. Sandy wanted to invite her friend, Lynn, to come, but she knew Lynn and her mother were shopping. Besides, Sandy wished to be alone to say good-bye to the tranquil pond and woods, which she had known all her life.

She meandered down Tyler's Hill, stepped into the lush, sweet-smelling woods, and walked straight to her pond. The bulldozers and chainsaws working in the near distance broke the normal tranquility of her beloved Tyler's Hill. Even so, it felt refreshing to get out of the hot sun and into the cool tree-canopied pond area. Sandy sat down, took off her shoes and socks, and let the prickly grass tickle her toes. A variety of colorful wildflowers dotted the grass. She picked a few, smelled them, and tucked them behind her ear. Wide-eyed, she stared into the pond; tadpoles darted back and forth. She studied them and noted they were still elongated. Thousands moved in unison. She plunged her jar into the water.

"Gotcha!" She scooped up her prize. A dozen or so tadpoles filled the jar. "I'm gonna watchcha guys change into frogs," she said as a big smile crossed her face. To prevent them from falling out, she screwed on the lid. "It's a good thing I made lots of holes. You'll breathe okay. Don't worry, you'll each have your own jar, when I getcha home." Setting her treasure beside her, she fell back into the grass, closed her eyes, and listened to the squirrels scurrying about and the gentle lapping of the water and whispered, "My own paradise!"

A couple of hours into her outing to Tyler's Hill, she was ready for her final walk through the fields. She put on her shoes, and picked up her tadpoles. She walked on the path out of the woods. Stopped. She turned in the opposite direction. She walked for about a mile until the path ended, and was about to turn around to go home when something beckoned her farther.

As she tromped through the woods, she pushed away the hanging branches. She scraped herself on several occasions, trying to walk around the overgrown thorny bushes. She finally came to a clearing and gasped. Her eyes became saucers. Her heart raced. "Wow! This is what the kids at school were talking about. It must be over a hundred years old. They said ghosts were inside!"

It was wooden-framed, with brown paint peeling off everywhere. Part of the roof had caved in. The front screen door was hanging off the hinges and the wooden porch was sagging. Sandy was determined to go inside. *I'm not scared,* she thought, clutching her tadpole jar to her chest. She stepped onto the rickety porch. "So, this is Miller's Haunted House," she said under her breath. Creaking noises suggested the porch might collapse. She twisted the doorknob. Locked. She pushed on the door. It didn't budge. She peered through the dirty windows and was surprised to see old, worn-down furniture, laden with years of dust. On one of the tables near the dilapidated sofa, she saw some ceramic pottery and an old, tattered, leather Bible, its cover surprisingly void of the dust the other items had collected.

"This is really old stuff," she whispered, with her nose pressed up against the glass-plated window. Her eyes studied the room. Talking to her tadpoles, she exclaimed, "Wow, look at that old photograph above the fireplace! Isn't she beautiful?" The bride in the picture had black, long hair, wore a satin wedding gown, and lovingly looked at her husband. In contrast, his angular-shaped face peered straight out from the photograph. "That's creepy." She suddenly thought she saw movement inside the room. Her body jumped and dropped the jar, which shattered, creating a writhing mess of glass and tadpoles on the porch.

She ran back through the thicket onto the cleared path. She finally stopped running when she reached the pond. She fell to her knees panting. Her head throbbed. *There was someone in the house. I'm sure of it. A ghost? Naw, there's no such thing. Well, whatever it was, it doesn't matter now, because the bulldozers will be coming soon.*

Sandy came out of the woods empty-handed and trudged back up Tyler's Hill to watch the bulldozers and lumberjacks do their work. She cried out, "Look what they've done to my woods! It's hideous!" At least four acres had been destroyed. Sandy saw her once-strong, sturdy oaks, magnificent maples, and towering pine trees lying helplessly on the ground. Some were slowly being lifted with a crane from their home to a huge flatbed truck. The newly cleared land looked stark and desolate. To Sandy, it seemed to call out to its "children" lying like helpless rubble on top of the flatbed truck. Choking back a sob, she sat and watched through a veil of tears.

I know it's only a few hours before the bulldozers reach my pond, she thought. Her face flushed red. Her mind twirled . . . *I gotta think of a way to save it! I just gotta!* No solution . . . Small perspiration beads formed in the indentation of her upper lip and across her brow. After several minutes, her eyes brightened. "I know what I'll do. I'll run in front of the bulldozers and stop 'em!" she shouted. "I dare 'em to mow me down!"

She raced down the hill. As she reached the bottom, a car horn blared, competing with the deafening bulldozers. She looked over and saw her father.

"Come on, dear, your mother has dinner on the table."

"But, Dad, I'm trying to save my pond! You've gotta help me!"

Mr. Lowenthal got out of his car and faced his daughter. He grasped her shoulders with a weak grin. "Look, dear, I know how much these woods and pond mean to you, but there's nothing we can do about it. I'm really sorry."

"But, Dad, you gotta do something!" She pulled away to watch the continuing onslaught.

"I wish I could, baby." He, too, watched as the bulldozers charged the woods.

"But you always know what to do. Always!" she said, as her arms flared in the air.

"It's out of my hands, sweetie." Mr. Lowenthal stepped closer to his daughter to brush away hair that had fallen into her face, revealing her bloodshot eyes.

"Just tell 'em to stop! They'll listen to you," pleaded Sandy, with her eyes still glued to the ongoing destruction.

"I'd like to, just to make you happy." A sad smile crossed his face. "But I'm afraid it wouldn't do any good." He led her to the car. As they walked, he took her hand and he felt her body trembling.

As the sun was sinking into the late afternoon skies, Sandy's mood sank into despair. The despair created a sensation of numbness, which seeped into her lower extremities, making it difficult for her to walk. Mr. Lowenthal opened the front passenger side door for his daughter. She slumped into the car, barely able to hold up her head. They drove home in silence.

When Sandy woke, she heard the bulldozers from her house. She stayed home and listened to the sounds from her bed. She cried into her pillow, as she lay listening to the distant drone of the bulldozers. She stopped listening when she became aware of other sounds that were growing louder—her stomach, growling from hunger! Sandy had been too upset to eat dinner last night. She jumped out of bed. "I'm starving."

She hurried into the kitchen and found her father reading the paper with a cup of coffee in his hand. "Dad, what are you doing home?"

"I'm not going to the hardware store today," he said, putting down his paper and coffee on the table.

"But, Dad, you never miss work." She sat down to face her dad at the kitchen table.

"That's true, that's true, and especially my busiest day of the week, Saturday."

"Who'll be at the store?"

"Your Uncle Bill said he'll be fine working the store with Simon today." A big smile spread across his face as he continued. "You see, last night I heard the weatherman say it's going to be 97 degrees and humid! Sounds like a beach day to me."

Sandy heaved a sigh. "I don't feel like going. Ask Frank and Linda to go."

"Your sister is working, and your brother spent last night at Jacky's house."

"Thanks, Dad, but I just wanna stay home today." She poured some milk into her cereal.

"Come on, my baby girl, we'll have a good time. Why don't you ask Lynn to come?" He kissed his daughter on the forehead and left the kitchen, leaving her alone to decide.

He was a man with endless patience. He had a handsome, oval-shaped face, with dark hair receding on top and strands of gray coloring his temples. Mr. Lowenthal had gentle brown eyes, and at age fifty, the few wrinkles that lined his forehead made him look dignified. He was the pillar of strength within the family—consistent, reliable, and hard working—a dedicated family man. A man of few words, his deeds spoke for him. Although he was not tall, he walked with an air of confidence, exuding dignity.

As Sandy ate her breakfast, she thought about what her dad said, and finally reached for the phone. "Hello," Lynn answered, sitting in her den watching television.

"Hey, Lynn, it's me, Sandy."

"What's goin' on?" She lowered the sound.

"You wanna go to Walled Lake today, with me and my dad?"

"Your dad's not working today?" She reached for the soda on top of the table and took a sip.

"Naw, he's feeling sorry for me." Sandy pushed the spoon into her cereal bowl.

"What for?" questioned Lynn.

"I'll tell ya at the beach."

"Okay. Let me ask my mom. Just hold on." Within a minute, Lynn was running back to the phone. "Yep, my mom said I can go!"

"All right, swell. We'll pick ya up in about an hour." She hung up and sprang from her chair to search for her bathing suit.

Lynn was one of Sandy's best friends; they had become inseparable since meeting in second grade. When they were together, they laughed until their bellies ached. Once, Lynn had Sandy laughing so hard she had a bladder control accident. With any other person in the world, Sandy would have been embarrassed, but with Lynn the situation turned into comedy.

The two adored each other like sisters, despite the marked differences between their appearances and personalities. Sandy was at least two inches shorter than Lynn and more muscular. Sandy was known to be more headstrong, persistent, and quick tempered. Lynn was more analytical, understanding, and cautious. Whereas they were both pretty girls, Lynn's blond hair and blue eyes, along with her lanky beauty, made her noticeable in a crowd. Lynn's mom thought her daughter was too skinny and was always trying to get her to eat. This was never Sandy's problem; she loved food. In fact, Sandy had a nickname within her family: the bottomless pit. Because she was so active, however, she burned off every calorie, looking fit and trim.

The girls enjoyed their beach day. They swam, lay out in the sand working on their tans, and ate hot dogs. They even entered the sand castle contest.

"Come on, Lynn, add some more over here," urged Sandy. "The contest will be over in less than a minute!"

"Okay . . ." and Lynn poured out the last bucket of sand. The girls feverishly worked on the last details to their sand castle, and then a whistle sounded.

"Contestants in the Walled Lake Daily Sand Castle Contest: Please stop and step away from your castles. The head lifeguard will choose the winner." As the lifeguard walked by all the castles and nearer to theirs, Lynn whispered to Sandy, "You'll think we'll win?"

"Of course! Ours is the best one here!"

No sooner than she spoke, the lifeguard pushed a blue flag into the sand next to the girls' work of art, and declared on his megaphone, "Sand Castle 22 is the winner!"

Sandy had forgotten the situation near Tyler's Hill while at the beach. She recalled it when late that evening she and her dad pulled into the driveway, and she was helping him take in the beach items. The painful memory washed over her, like a huge wave, making her feel helpless and she thought, *I'm never gonna go back to Tyler's Hill. Never!*

CHAPTER 2

"A New Friend?"

Sandy, a sixth grader now, was well into the school year, and in early January turned twelve. In the fall, she was voted president of Student Council. She, the other student council members, and the entire school were involved in a charity project—raising money through bake sales to help a needy foreign college student finish her teaching degree at a local university. Their goal was to raise a thousand dollars by the end of the school year, and they were well on their way. By the completion of their fourth sale, Sandy was happy to report to the class that they had already made five hundred dollars, leaving them plenty of time to plan for more. Mrs. MacKenzie, Sandy's sixth grade teacher, thanked Sandy for the report and then said, "Now, I have some information to share with you before you're dismissed to begin the weekend. On Monday, we will have a new student in class. Her name is Beth Fine. I'm telling you now so you can think of ways of welcoming her into our classroom."

Glenn, the class clown, yelled out, "Why don't we proclaim it a holiday, and cancel school?"

All the students chimed in, "Yeah, that's a great idea!"

Mrs. MacKenzie, always able to handle a joke replied, "I know we're all getting excited about winter vacation, but we have to sit tight for another week."

Jill, pointing out the window, exclaimed, "Look, everybody!"

Finally, the first snowflakes of the winter season had arrived, and it was coming down fast and furious. Everyone quickly sprang from their desks to watch out the side windows that stretched across the entire length of the classroom.

The children's eyes sparkled in amazement as they watched the snow fall. Sandy, like most children from the Midwest, adored winter. It meant building snowmen, organizing snowball fights, sledding down Tyler's Hill, and school closings. The children were mesmerized by the snow's quiet beauty until they heard the dismissal bell ring, signaling the beginning of their weekend freedom. Mrs. MacKenzie called out over the commotion as all the children rushed to pull on their winter coats and gloves, "Remember the school rule. No throwing snowballs!" Everyone agreed they wouldn't. "All right, as soon as everyone is quiet and in a straight line, I can excuse you," said Mrs. MacKenzie. All the children, anxious to get outside to breathe the frosty air and start their weekend, were quiet and in a straight line within thirty seconds. "Have a great . . ." and before Mrs. MacKenzie finished speaking, her students charged down the hall like a stampede.

Mrs. MacKenzie's attempt to slow them down was hopeless. Chris, the first outside, immediately tested the white, moist substance beneath his feet. "Hey, it's great packing snow!" In an instant chaos broke out—snowballs flying everywhere. Sandy was hit several times, even as she tried dodging them. She felt lucky to live close to school, and was safely inside her house only seconds before a snowball crashed onto her porch, missing her by a hair's breadth. She raced to the basement to get her sled and head to Tyler's Hill, but couldn't find it.

Anxiously, she yelled up the stairs, "Mom, I can't find my sled anywhere!"

Her mother replied, "Dad put it in the attic."

And then Sandy gulped. She remembered promising not to return to Tyler's Hill.

"Don't worry," her mom said, "Dad can get it down for you when he comes home from work."

"Nah, that's okay. I really don't need it."

The next morning Sandy went to the living room window, and found it was frosted over with snow piled up on the ledges, covering part of the glass, making it impossible to see outside. Hurriedly, she used her fingernails to scratch out a view. *Wow, it must be at least eight inches of snow out there*, she thought. It was a winter wonderland, with sunlight bouncing off the white, powdery stuff in every direction. *You can't even see my street, because of the huge snow drifts. This is awesome!* She saw the snow plows busily at work, trying to clear the roads so cars could get through. She saw dozens of her neighbors outside shoveling their sidewalks and driveways. Sandy thought to herself, *If this had been a weekday, school would've been cancelled, for sure!* As she continued peering through the scratched out window section, she saw kids pulling their sleds behind them as they trudged through the snow, heading in the direction of the school. Sandy was anxious. She desperately wanted to get her sled and join the other kids, but she was torn. She said she'd never go back. Then the telephone rang; it was Lynn.

"Sandy, I'll meet you at Tyler's Hill to go sledding!"

"My sled is up in the attic." Sandy gulped and bit her lip.

Sandy's dad, who was drinking his morning coffee and reading his paper at the kitchen table, overheard his daughter. "No, it isn't, dear. I brought it down from the attic last night and put it outside."

"Lynn, I'll call you back." Sandy hung up the phone and looked at her dad. "Dad, I wanna go, but I don't wanna go."

"Because of how they changed the area?"

Sandy slumped her shoulders. "I said I'd never go back."

"Dear, we all say and do things when we hurt that we really don't mean."

"But, Dad—"

"It's okay to change your mind. Why don't you get your sled and join your friends at Tyler's Hill."

Sandy threw her arms around her dad's neck, planting a big kiss on his cheek. "You're the best dad in the world!" In the next instant, she was putting on her boots, jacket, hat, and gloves and dashing to get her sled to join Lynn and the other children at Tyler's Hill.

Because the hill was steep and slippery, the climb was a struggle. When Sandy finally reached the top, she could not believe her eyes. What once had been her beloved refuge—her pond, in its hearty woods with their delectable sights and smells had vanished. In its place stood row after row of houses—brick two-story colonial homes with attached garages. She had known that this would happen, but seeing it for the first time left her feeling sick to her stomach and a bit dizzy.

Sandy's eyes fixated on the new subdivision until finally one of the kids yelled, "Come on, Sandy, take yer turn! You're holding up the show!" She plunged onto her sled, gripping the cross bar with her head hanging over the front edge, and her feet stretched behind. She went zooming down, but before she could stop herself, she was speeding into another child coming down the hill. The two sleds collided.

Their riders were thrown off their sleds and started tumbling down the hill together, landing on top of each other. Their breath was knocked out of them. Sandy was the first to get to her feet.

"Are you okay?" she asked the other girl, a bit shaken from the accident. "I'm so sorry. My sled got out of control. I wasn't paying attention as well as I should've been."

The girl got up, a bit bruised, with no apparent cuts, just a scrape or two and started brushing off the snow. "Yeah. I'm okay, now."

Sandy asked, "What's your name?"

The girl replied, "Beth."

"I'm Sandy. It was really stupid of me, Beth. I was thinking about . . ."

Beth cut her off, "Don't worry about it. I'm really okay. Let's just go back up and do it right this time."

The girls, both aching a little, but ready for the challenge, trudged back up Tyler's Hill.

Beth yelled, "Come on, Sandy, I betcha I can beat you up the hill."

"We'll see about that."

And the two girls, huffing and puffing in the winter air, managed to pull themselves up Tyler's Hill at the same time. Once at the top, Beth, catching her breath, laughed, "I promise not to crash into you, if you promise not to crash into me."

"That's a deal," agreed Sandy. The two girls raced each other to the bottom, as the winter sun in a cloudless sky seemed to cheer them on. Beth declared victory, although Sandy didn't agree.

"Hey, it was a tie," insisted Sandy.

"All right, I won't argue with you," said Beth as she started to climb the hill again.

Sandy was a bit of a daredevil and was ready for more adventure, shouting, "Beth, now you wanna try something really fun?"

"Sure!"

"All right, let's go down on one sled together!"

"That could be a little dangerous."

"Hey, it'll make us go ten times faster. It's really fun. Come on, try it, Beth!"

Beth finally agreed, although rather reluctantly, and before she had time to change her mind, the two girls were flying down Tyler's Hill—going faster than they'd ever gone before. When they reached the bottom, Sandy touted, "I told you it was gonna be fun! Come on, Beth, let's do it again!"

"That was just a little too fast for me," said Beth, as she pulled her red ski cap further down her forehead and got up from the sled facing her new friend.

"Oh, just once more," pleaded Sandy.

Before Beth could answer, Lynn finally arrived and called, "Sandy."

"Where've you been, Lynn?" Sandy's nose was bright red from the cold and her face looked windblown.

"My mom asked me to help her bring in the groceries. Sorry I'm late."

"That's okay." Sandy adjusted her scarf and pulled her sled to the side. "Lynn, I want you to meet Beth. Beth, this is my good friend Lynn. We've known each other since second grade."

"Hi," said Lynn, with a smile and welcoming eyes. "Where do you live, Beth?"

Beth, rubbing her mittened hands together to keep warm, stopped and turned to point. "In those new houses over there. You'll both have to come visit," said Beth cheerfully. "We moved in a few days ago."

Sandy was stunned. Her eyelids flared opened, revealing the whites of her eyeballs. Her heart started racing. She could have agreed to a lot of things. However, visiting one of the homes that had destroyed her woods and pond was like being asked to stick a knife in her own back. Going to Beth's home would be like fraternizing with the enemy. *No, I'm never gonna go to Beth's house!* she thought. Sandy felt awkward and immediately wanted to flee. Suddenly, she felt the cold penetrate her bones. Finally, she managed to sputter, "Well . . . all I know . . . I'm freezing out here! I've gotta go. I mean, I'm really freezing!"

Lynn, surprised by Sandy's peculiar behavior, quickly said, "But, Sandy, I just got here. Are you okay? You're acting kinda' weird."

Nervously, Sandy quipped, "Yeah, I'm fine. I'm just freezing to death." Her lips started to shiver. "See ya' guys later." Before Lynn could object, Sandy was hurrying away, pulling her sled behind her, leaving tracks in the snow that showed her anger as she headed home.

Beth gave a puzzled look to Lynn, and Lynn, feeling embarrassed over Sandy's strange behavior, shrugged her shoulders saying, "I really don't know what's bugging her today!"

CHAPTER 3

Secrets

Sandy always looked forward to returning to school at the end of the weekend. After two days of playing with friends, watching television, and going out for Sunday dinner with her family, Sandy was usually ready to "hit the books." This Sunday, Sandy's dad had taken the family to the usual place—great-uncle Sam's Delicatessen. Sandy adored this restaurant. It had an aroma like no other, pungent smells of garlic and onions clung to the air, and large booths, upholstered with thick red leather cushions, that Sandy's bottom comfortably sank into. Not to mention, the restaurant had her favorite foods: matzo ball soup, corn beef sandwiches with French fries, her great-uncle's scrumptious hamburgers, and, of course, the most delicious desserts, like cheesecake, strudel, or halawa.

Sandy's mom always ordered the halawa for dessert; her father always got the strudel, served warm. Sandy's brother, Frank, went with chocolate sundaes with hot fudge on top, as did her sister, Linda. Sandy was always torn between ordering the strudel, like her dad, or cheesecake. Tonight, she decided on cheesecake with strawberries on top, because she knew she'd get to taste the strudel, since her dad always offered her a bit of his. "Sandy, would you like some of my warm apple strudel?"

"Thanks, not tonight, Dad. The cheesecake is enough for me." But Sandy's dad noticed that she hardly touched her dinner, and only one bite of the cheesecake was missing. He knew something was on his daughter's mind. However, before he could ask Sandy if there was a problem, great-uncle Sam, whose deeply creased forehead showed his age, came forward from the kitchen to speak with the family. He had a great, thick Eastern European accent: his "th" sounded like a "d", and his "w" came out sounding like a "v". He had sparkling blue eyes, and pure white hair, with endless waves.

"Oh, you're eating late dis evening, Ben. You and Ruth usually bring da family in by six."

"I was working on the tenth-of-the-month bills," answered Mr. Lowenthal.

"I know how dat can be. Vhen you own your own business, dere's always vork and bills to pay, but how vonderful to know de Kinder are growing up here, in America." And he took the opportunity to pinch Sandy's cheek, lovingly, shake Frank's hand, kindly kiss Linda's forehead, and pay a compliment to his niece, Mrs. Lowenthal.

"And to think, Sam, we're alive and well in America, all because of a dead horse!" exclaimed Mr. Lowenthal.

"No, Ben, you've been married to my lovely niece, Ruth, for seventeen years and I never heard dis story!"

"Well, it's all true just because of a dead horse. You see, Uncle Sam, my father was a traveling salesman in the old country. He'd go from town to town selling pots and pans, and other household items with his two strong, burly workhorses. He'd be gone the whole week, traveling long distances to sell his wares. But he always came back for the Sabbath. One late Friday afternoon before the Sabbath, my siblings and I were helping our mama clean the house. I opened the door to sweep the dirt out and saw my papa approaching with his big wagon, but just one horse. He wore the saddest face that I'd ever seen on my papa. I raced down the road, climbed onto the wagon and asked, "Papa, where's Grey-lad?"

"G-d had other plans for him, Beryl, my dear son."

"That Sabbath dinner was one of our saddest. Usually, after Mama lit the candles and all the prayers were said, Papa was filled with stories about the places he'd been, the people he had met, but not that evening—his mind was on other things. The next day we walked as a family to the synagogue and prayed. But I noticed my father was *dovening* (praying) harder than usual. He wrapped himself more completely in his *tallis* (prayer shawl) than I'd ever seen before. I was barely able to see his face. Even after arriving home from the synagogue he was unusually quiet. Only after the sun had set on Saturday and the Sabbath was over, did he speak. He spoke directly to his wife, with his five children listening."

"Regina, my dear wife, I've decided—our children were only born in Europe, but they will live in America!"

"Before my mama could protest, my papa held up his hand to stop her. He continued by saying, 'I have money to buy another horse or buy passage to America, where I can live with my brother, and start a new life for us . . . a better life with more opportunities. After I've saved enough money to start a business, I'll bring you and the Kinder over. But my children will live in America!'"

"Vhat year, Ben?" asked Uncle Sam.

"My papa came to America in 1921, and seven years later in '28, we joined him. Those who stayed went up in smoke—in Auschwitz."

Great Uncle Sam was shaking his head. "G-d works in mysterious ways. Thank goodness that horse died!"

"Amen to that!" declared Mr. Lowenthal.

Sandy usually listened intently when her father and great-uncle spoke, especially when they discussed the old country. But tonight, she was absorbed in her own thoughts. *Just great, there are three other sixth-grade classrooms, and the new girl is gonna be in my class. Well, she's not gonna be my friend, or any of the other kids living in the new subdivision. It's because of them that they destroyed my woods and pond.* Even though a small section of the woods remained, she vowed to be only cordial to Beth, but not her friend. She refused to become a friend of the enemy.

The next morning, Mrs. MacKenzie stood in the front of the room near the blackboard, looking refreshed after her weekend and wearing a plaid wool suit said, "Class, I want to introduce you to Beth Fine. Please welcome Beth to her first day at Tyler School." Sandy looked up from the book she was reading and noticed that Beth, standing next to Mrs. MacKenzie, had a head full of attractive, thick, black curls, which Sandy hadn't noticed the day they were sledding together, because Beth had been wearing a tight-fitting ski cap. Beth started touching and twisting her curls around her fingers, a habit she had when she was nervous. The teacher continued, "I'd like to take the next twenty minutes or so to have each of you introduce yourself to Beth and let her know a little about yourself. We'll start with this row. Kenneth, you begin, please."

Kenneth, the tallest boy in the class, stood up. "My name is Kenneth Edward Dwight, but everyone calls me Ken, except Mrs. MacKenzie. Anyway, my favorite thing is baseball and I'm gonna play in the pros when I grow up. And, of course, I'll be playing this summer, so you can all come and watch me. I guess that's it."

"Thank you, Kenneth. Judy, you're next." Now it was Sandy's turn to be nervous, because it was her turn to speak, after Judy. Sandy was grateful that Judy was speaking because she always had a lot to say and spoke very slowly; this gave her time to think. In fact, it was quite normal for Mrs. Mackenzie to cut Judy off in mid-sentence, to give other children a chance to voice their opinions. This morning was the first time Sandy had seen Beth, since Saturday's embarrassing "escape" from Tyler's Hill.

Sandy prayed that Beth didn't remember her, and reassured herself, thinking, *Of course Beth wouldn't, I was wearing my winter coat and hat. Certainly she wouldn't recognize me now—in my school clothes.*

"All right, Judy, I think Beth now has a full understanding . . ."

"But, Mrs. MacKenzie, I haven't finished telling Beth about all my pets!" protested Judy.

"Perhaps you could share this information with Beth at lunch time. All right, Sandy, what information are you going to share about yourself with Beth?"

Beth, recognizing Sandy exclaimed, "I know you! We met sledding at Tyler's Hill on Saturday."

How many shades of red Sandy was turning she wasn't certain, but if escaping from the classroom had been an option, she'd have taken it. Sandy was at a loss for words. She was groping to say something clever like, *Yes, we had the occasion to enjoy a fine day of sledding down Tyler's Hill. It was a pleasure to meet you.* But instead, she was silent; tongue-tied. Mrs. MacKenzie saw that she needed assistance. "I'm delighted you two met sledding. I'm sure you both enjoyed it. Sandy, why don't you tell Beth about your involvement with Student Council and the fundraising project? Maybe Beth wants to get involved?"

Sandy thought to herself, *Saved by Mrs. MacKenzie! Now, why didn't I think of that?* Sandy stood up by her desk and the words tumbled out. "Beth, next week the school is having a Bake Sale fundraiser for a needy college student. If you wanna help, you just need to bake—or ask your mom to bake—a dozen brownies."

"It's a great idea," said Beth. "I'd love to help."

"Thank you, Sandy," Mrs. MacKenzie said. Lynn was next. Sandy didn't hear what Lynn said, or for that matter, what any of her other classmates said, because she was still feeling the effects of being so embarrassed.

During the next week, Sandy was quite involved with her other schoolmates in preparing for the bake sale. She helped to write the publicity and get the notices passed out to the other grades. It was now the day before the sale and she thought, *Shucks, I've got a problem. We just don't have enough desserts. I'm gonna have to ask them for more baked goods*, and she approached Judy first.

"Gee, I'm sorry, Sandy, my mom said she'd bake for the next one. She has to be at my brother's hockey game tonight."

The students had valid excuses as to why they were not bringing baked goods tomorrow. However, this created great consternation for Sandy, since she was the main organizer of the project. Without enough baked goods to sell, the school wouldn't meet its charity goal.

Beth noticed Sandy approaching many of the students and overheard the conversation. Wanting to be helpful, she walked over to Sandy.

"What do you need for tomorrow's sale?"

Feeling quite relieved that Beth was willing to help, Sandy blurted out, "Everything! Do you think you and your mom could make brownies and chocolate chip cookies?"

"Well, I usually bake. My mom . . . well, my sisters help me, but tonight, they're studying for exams. Why don't you come and bake with me?"

Now, for the second time in Sandy's life she was tongue-tied. Her desire to go to Beth's was as low as the baked goods inventory for tomorrow's sale. Sandy felt desperate about the situation. Beth waited uncomfortably for an answer to her question. Sandy thought to herself with pursed lips, *There are twenty-nine other students in class besides me. Why can't Beth ask one of them?* Then she had a flash of how much fun she and Beth had had sledding together. Sandy once again saw Beth begin twisting her curls with her fingers.

"Oh, Sandy, you're probably too busy with other things getting ready for tomorrow's sale."

"No . . . no . . .Beth. I can help you. We can bake together," Sandy finally managed to say with feigned enthusiasm.

"Great!" exclaimed Beth. "What about coming over right after school?"

"Sure, that'll be fine," Sandy said quietly under her breath. "I'll just have to call my mom when I get to your house."

Most children, including Sandy, were ready to leave school by the end of the day. They had had enough. But, today, Sandy was anxious about the dismissal bell ringing; for that sounded the alarm for her to go somewhere she'd rather not, and to be with a person with whom she really didn't want to be. Then she remembered her father's saying when situations look bleak, "It could be worse." Sandy had to admit this was a good philosophy. So, with a big gulp and her stomach performing like an acrobat, she started walking home with Beth.

For the first time, Sandy entered the new subdivision, viewing the big brick colonial homes up close. Her stomach was not feeling any better. She thought to herself, *It must be nice to live in one of them.* After walking five blocks, they arrived at

Beth's house. She took out her key and opened the door. The two entered the spacious foyer.

Beth yelled out, "I'm home," as she set her keys on the white marble table, situated in the middle of the brightly lit foyer.

Beth's older sister, Karen, yelled from upstairs, "Beth, I'm studying. I'll be down later to cook dinner."

As the girls were taking their winter clothes off, Sandy's eyes surveyed her surroundings and she thought, *Wow, I've never been in a house so beautiful and clean! Gee, my house is never this clean, and my house is so small in comparison to Beth's.*

Beth interrupted her thoughts. "Sandy, let's put our books and coats in the family room and then eat a snack before we start baking."

Sandy followed Beth into the family room, looked out the sliding glass doors, and froze. She blinked her eyes twice, making certain she was not imagining the view.

"It's my pond!" she shouted. Sandy, elated, quickly opened the doors and ran outside without her coat, even though the thermometer attached to the birdhouse indicated it was 32 degrees Fahrenheit.

Beth shouted after her, "Where are you going?" and ran to get her coat to come after Sandy. "Sandy, what's wrong?" she asked, confused by Sandy's erratic behavior.

Sandy's surprise at learning that "her pond" was not destroyed was as unexpected as the winter sparrow perched overhead, who came suddenly soaring directly above the girls' heads, singing a song, as in celebration of the joyous occasion.

"Beth, why didn't you tell me the day we met at Tyler's Hill that my pond is in your backyard?"

"Your pond?" Beth said, with a quizzical expression on her face, zipping her parka.

"I mean, now it's yours. But this is the pond I've adored since . . . well, since I can remember about things. But I thought for months the bulldozers had destroyed it, when they built all the new houses. Do you have any idea how upset I've been over this?" said Sandy.

"No. But now that I know, consider it your pond, too. I love it, just like you! In fact, my dad is getting it ready so I can skate on it this weekend. Wanna' skate with me?"

Sandy was so ecstatic she still couldn't believe it. This was the best news she had had in months and she gleefully chimed, "You betcha! I'd like to see anyone stop me!"

"We'll have a blast, but now I've got to get you back in the house; I'm freezing with my coat on!" insisted Beth. Sandy barely noticed the cold. She still was staring in disbelief at "her" pond. Beth yelled, "Come on, Sandy. Remember, there's a bake sale tomorrow."

"Yeah, I'm coming," beamed Sandy.

The girls walked back into the house, and Beth pulled all of her baking supplies out of the cupboards. There was everything the girls needed. Beth had several packets of brownie mix and all the ingredients for chocolate chip cookies. She proceeded to take out the necessary mixing bowls, cookie sheets, glass baking dishes and wooden spoons. Within two and a half hours, the girls managed to bake four dozen chocolate chip cookies and four dozen brownies. Whereas the baked good items were lined up neatly on the counter, everything else in the kitchen lay in disarray. The girls were better bakers than cleaners. All the kitchen cabinets were open. Pots and pans, dirty spoons, knives and utensils were everywhere.

Beth's oldest sister, Karen, walked into the kitchen and upon seeing the mess screamed, "Beth, what in the world are you doing!"

Beth, trying to calm her sister down, said matter of factly, "We're baking for the Bake Sale tomorrow."

Red-faced, Beth's sister yelled, "Did you ask permission? You know Mom . . ."

"I asked Dad and he said it was okay," said Beth, angrily, cutting off her sister in mid-sentence.

"Well, it's not okay with me!" snapped Karen. "I'm the one making dinner tonight, and look at this mess! Now, I'll never get dinner done before Dad gets home!"

Just then a weak voice coming from upstairs was heard. "Girls, what's wrong?"

"See, now you've woken Mom! Beth, you're such an idiot!"

"You woke her! You're yelling so loud you could wake up a dead person!" barked Beth.

Sandy felt awkward in the middle of a family fight. Especially a family she didn't know that well, but feeling she had to say something since she contributed to making the mess, she turned to face Beth's sister.

"We'll start cleaning up right now, and on the double!" Sandy started immediately washing the mixing bowls.

Within a moment she heard Beth scream, "Mom!"

There, standing in the kitchen doorway with her housecoat on, looking frail and ill, was Beth's mother.

"Mom, you need to get back into bed," urged Beth's sister. "You know what the doctor said . . ."

"I know, dear. But I heard my girls yelling . . ." and Mrs. Fine put her hand on the kitchen table to help balance herself.

"It's okay, Mom, we've got it handled. We're just doing a little baking for Beth's bake sale tomorrow," replied Karen.

Mrs. Fine finally saw Sandy standing by the sink and turned to her youngest daughter.

"Beth, is this a friend from school?" and her hand started to tremble on the kitchen table, so she quickly used her other hand.

"Yeah, Mom. This is Sandy Lowenthal."

"Hi, Mrs. Fine," said Sandy. "Sorry we woke you."

"No problem, girls. I'll just go back upstairs now and rest," said Mrs. Fine weakly.

Mrs. Fine slowly climbed the stairs to her room and the girls continued cleaning the kitchen. There was a solemn quiet that came over all three of them. With the cleanup finished, Sandy telephoned her mother, requesting a ride home, knowing she wasn't allowed to walk alone on a cold winter's night. As Sandy waited in the foyer, Beth continued to be subdued, and began twisting her curls, fast, and her body began fidgeting. Sandy sensed that Beth wanted to tell her something important, but was reluctant. Finally, Beth broke the uncomfortable silence.

"Did I ever tell you why my family moved to Michigan?"

"No," answered Sandy, curiously, as she looked intently at Beth, noticing her long eyelashes for the first time, but sensing the moment's significance.

"My dad heard about a doctor who could help people who are ill."

Sandy moved closer to Beth, an inch from her nose, in order to hear Beth because she continued in a whisper.

"I mean very, very ill—with cancer." Beth's gaze fell to the floor, and she paused creating a long silence.

Sandy thought she heard Beth's heart pounding in rhythm with her own. Beth finally managed to collect her emotions.

"Sandy, my dad is doing everything he can for my mom. Please, don't tell anyone at school about this. I don't want people to know; it's just none of their business!"

"I won't say a word about this. I promise."

Beth was dissatisfied with this answer. "That's not enough! Say, Deep Talk."

"What?" questioned Sandy, not understanding what her friend meant.

"Deep Talk means it's more than a promise," stated Beth, excitedly, with her eyes blazing. "When two friends say Deep Talk over something, it means they are guarding a sacred secret together. If one tells, then the friendship is instantly broken, and never to be again. So you see it's much, much more than a promise! Sandy, to say Deep Talk, we must connect our arms, look deeply into each other's eyes, and at the exact same second say, Deep Talk."

"Okay. I'll do it," she said. Her body was rigid at first, never having done a ritual like this, but as soon as she locked her eyes and arms onto Beth's, she relaxed.

The girls counted in unison—"One, two . . ." and in the next breath, pledged, Deep Talk to each other. Sandy immediately sensed a bond with another human being she had never known before.

Sandy wanted to say more to Beth, like how sorry she was about her mother's illness, but she heard her mom blowing the horn. Sandy quickly zipped up her jacket and ran out into the cold of the night, a contrast to the glowing warmth she felt within. Sandy sat quietly as she drove home with her mom, listening to the hum of the engine. Her eyes glanced out the side door window and up at the nighttime sky. She noticed the moon. It was full and bright, illuminating the street on which they traveled home. She studied the myriad of twinkling stars and spotted the Big Dipper, feeling a tingling sensation inside, making her realize she had just gone through a very powerful and meaningful experience with her new friend. She vowed to keep the Deep Talk pledge, protecting Beth by guarding her family's secret. Sandy knew about family secrets because Sandy's family had one too.

CHAPTER 4

Rituals

"One hundred ninety-eight, one hundred ninety-nine, two hundred dollars and fifty-nine cents!" shouted Sandy as she finished counting the proceeds from the bake sale. "Beth, that's the most we've ever made!"

"Come on," insisted Beth, "let's go tell the class!"

Both girls ran into Mrs. MacKenzie's classroom shouting, "We made more than $200!" Hearing this news, Mrs. Mackenzie told the class how proud she was of them working together and that their efforts will help a fortunate student achieve her educational dreams to be able to succeed in life.

Glenn Schwartz, the class clown, with chocolate smeared over his face, jumped up from his seat. "Personally, I thought the chocolate chip cookies were the best!" The other children started laughing uncontrollably.

"Glenn, why don't you go to the bathroom and take a look in the mirror," chided Mrs. MacKenzie, obviously annoyed by Glenn disrupting the class. The teacher tried getting the students to settle back down. "Children, we've just a few more minutes before dismissal. I need your attention. Please write your homework assignment down, which I've written on the blackboard."

Kate, another student in the classroom, groaned, "Forty fraction problems. I'll be up all night!"

"Calm down, Kate, it's not all for tonight," assured Mrs. MacKenzie. "The math assignment is due in two days because I've also given you one chapter in social studies to read for this evening."

After the dismissal bell sounded, Beth, bundled up in her winter attire and carrying her books in her arms, approached Sandy.

"You're great at fractions, Sandy; I could sure use some help. Do you mind if I come over to work on math?"

"You mean now? You wanna come today?" Sandy asked nervously, as she was putting on her mittens and preparing herself for the walk home.

"Yeah, today," replied Beth, seeming annoyed by Sandy's hesitancy.

"You can't."

"Just for an hour," pleaded Beth.

"I'm busy. I've drama class tonight."

"You told me drama is on Mondays. This is Wednesday," persisted Beth.

"Look, Beth, I can't have you over today because . . ."

"Never mind. I don't need your help anyway!" Beth retorted, and abruptly turned away to walk home, feeling hurt and rejected.

Sandy called after her, but Beth ignored the calls. Sandy walked home feeling angry. She wanted to tell Beth the truth about why she couldn't come over, but felt too ashamed. As Sandy headed home, she thought, *Maybe today, when I get home, the house will be clean, and I can call Beth to come over . . .* She held on and on to that thought, thinking that it would help.

She entered her house. "Look at this place, it's a mess!" she exclaimed.

Papers, books, and pens were all over the living room, and the television was blaring. When she walked into the kitchen, the dirty dishes were piled high in the sink, creating a foul smell. Cupboard doors were wide open with cereal boxes and packages of nonperishable foods stacked dangerously close to the edges of the shelves. Sandy sat at the kitchen table.

"Jeez, I can't even eat a snack without these cereal boxes and dirty bowls in the way!" and she pushed these items to the side in order to create enough space to eat the peanut butter and jelly sandwich that she'd made.

Her mom was doing laundry downstairs, and when she heard Sandy in the kitchen, she came up to give her daughter a hug.

But Sandy didn't hug her mother back. Instead, Sandy lashed out, "I can't even bring friends here, it's disgusting!" And before Mrs. Lowenthal could answer, Sandy ran into her bedroom and slammed the door.

After ten minutes of lying on her bed feeling sorry for herself, she abruptly sat up, grabbing the pink princess phone on the table between the twin beds and dialed Beth's number.

After two rings Beth answered. "Hello."

"I'm sorry about this afternoon."

"It's okay," replied Beth.

"No, it's not okay. How about coming to my house after school tomorrow and we'll work on the math?"

"Great! The assignment isn't due until Friday," said Beth, "See ya' tomorrow."

"See ya'," answered Sandy, and quickly put the phone back on the receiver. She sprang off her bed and made her way through the house picking up the mess, dusting and vacuuming. When she got to the kitchen, Mrs. Lowenthal was already working on the dishes piled in the sink. Sandy helped clean off the kitchen table. Within two hours the house was starting to take shape. Sandy saved her bedroom for last, knowing her sister, Linda, who shared the room with her, would help straighten it up.

Sandy liked sharing a bedroom with her big sister, for it allowed her to obtain privileged information about Linda's social life. Since Linda was seven years older than Sandy, in her freshman year at a local college, and living at home, Sandy was getting her own "college education," about the "birds and the bees."

Linda was into the dating scene and received a lot of telephone calls from the opposite sex. This played havoc on the one phone line in the house. Mrs. Lownethal always complained about never being able to make a call or receive any from her friends. In order to keep some peace in the house, Mr. Lowenthal had had a second telephone line installed in Linda and Sandy's bedroom when Linda turned sixteen, two years ago.

Linda told her male friends, "Call me when my little sister is asleep, around 10:00 p.m." Actually, though Sandy was asleep at 10:00 p.m., the telephone ring always woke her. She pretended to be sleeping, so she could hear what her sister said. When the phone rang last night she overheard, "Daniel, I wish you were here tonight. I miss you so much. When can we see each other again?"

"Yeak," Sandy said to herself, listening to the conversation as she pulled the blankets over her head. She thought they were getting carried away with this entire dating ritual.

While Sandy was cleaning their bedroom, Linda came charging into the room like a bolt of lighting.

"Sandy!" she yelled. "You have to help me. Daniel will be here to pick me up in one hour to help me with my photography class! I'm gonna take a quick shower and wash my hair. When I'm done, get both hair dryers out, to help me dry my hair. I don't want to be late!"

"Sure, I'll help. Did you notice the house?" inquired Sandy.

"Looks great. Mom clean it?"

"Well, I did most of it," Sandy stated proudly. "Now, I'm working on our room."

As Linda was preparing for her shower, Sandy questioned, "So, you're gonna study photography with Daniel tonight?" pretending that she hadn't overheard their conversation last night.

"Yeah," Linda replied. "Daniel is a great artist. I'll have to take you to his studio so you can see some of his work."

"That would be swell!" Sandy replied, as she went along picking up clothes from the bedroom floor.

Linda rushed into the bathroom. Sandy continued to straighten the room, and to get out the hair dryers as her sister had requested. Sandy actually didn't like Daniel. He may have been a great photographer, and from Linda's perspective a great kisser, but Sandy thought Daniel was arrogant. He never said one word to Sandy when he came to pick up Linda. Sandy always said, "Hi," but Daniel just ignored her and spoke impatiently. "Is Linda ready?" And Sandy always answered, "Almost." But that was a lie. Linda was never almost ready. She was slow as molasses. She took forever getting ready to go out on a date. So Daniel sat in the living room and waited and waited. The more impatient Daniel became, the more Sandy was pleased, feeling some sense of satisfaction for Daniel's rude behavior toward her. Of course, this was the perfect opportunity for Mr. and Mrs. Lowenthal to get to "know" the boy who was taking their firstborn out. It gave them a chance to determine whether or not he was good enough for their daughter.

However, Sandy wished Linda would see more of Robert. She liked Robert much better than Daniel. Robert was a pre-med student, who attended the same college as Linda. Robert was friendly. Every time he came to the house to pick up Linda, and while he waited, he told funny stories to Sandy and made her laugh. The only problem with Robert was that Sandy never heard Linda say at the end of their late night telephone conversations, "I love you," as she did with Daniel. Sandy, though she knew Linda was only eighteen and marriage was still quite in the distance for her, still had to do something about making sure she got a brother-in-law she liked. But that project had to wait for another time.

When the bedroom was finally cleaned up, Sandy plunked herself down on her twin bed, admiring her brightly colored bedroom and its beautiful wallpaper. It was just two years earlier when Linda was turning sixteen, that she had said to her baby sister, "Sandy, Dad gave me three hundred dollars to redecorate our bedroom, as part of my sweet sixteen gift. We can change the paint color, get wallpaper, carpeting . . .we can really make this drab looking room into something! What do ya' say?" Sandy, then only nine years old, thought it was the most exciting news she'd ever heard—they were going to redecorate their bedroom. And do it together.

Sandy absolutely adored her older sister. In Sandy's eyes, her older sister was like the queen bee; she could do no wrong. She was smart, beautiful, and very purposeful. The process of redecorating started out easy enough when Sandy asked, "What color will it be?"

Linda had it all figured out and declared, "Pink and orange!"

"Wow," Sandy replied, "pink and orange! That'll be beautiful!" Linda could've said yellow and black, and that, too, would have been fine for Sandy, because this was a project the two sisters were going to be doing together—and that is all that mattered to Sandy. Picking out the paint was simple, since Mr. Lowenthal owned the best hardware store in Detroit. Linda decided on a soft pink for three of the bedroom walls and the forth wall would be wallpaper, yet to be found. Since Mr. Lowenthal didn't sell wallpaper, the girls had to go to home decorating stores in search of the right one.

For several weeks, on Saturdays, Linda and Sandy visited stores, seeking the perfect design. It became their Saturday ritual. Most nine-year-olds would be bored out of their minds with this intensive search process, but not Sandy. Driving around with her older sister, who recently had gotten her license, was about the coolest thing Sandy could be doing. This particular Saturday, the two sisters had been to at least six locations, and Linda still hadn't found what she was looking for. Sandy and Linda must have looked through at least a hundred wallpaper books, but the problem was none had the color combination of pink and orange.

Lily's Wallpaper Center was the sisters' last stop of the day. Sandy was getting tired and so was Linda. The girls walked into the store and found it filled with people looking through the stacks of wallpaper books. "Okay, Sandy, you know the ritual, only these six are for bedrooms. You go through these three, and I'll look at the other three. Now, remember, we're looking for a flower pattern that is bright pink and orange." How could Sandy forget? They'd been doing this for weeks. Each sister methodically flipped the pages in their books, one after another, but to no avail. The pink and orange–flowered wallpaper was not to be found.

Exhausted, the two sisters were about to leave and head home, when another customer put down a wallpaper book on the table and it caught Sandy's eye.

"Look, Linda!" Sandy ran to it. On its cover was written, "Wallpaper for Dining Rooms."

Linda was amazed and said, "This is exactly what I was looking for!" The book's cover featured Linda's first choice. The background of the paper was white, with thin, pale pink pinstripes running down it, with lovely intertwining brightly colored pink and orange flowers, overlaying the stripes.

Sandy was now lying on her bed happily gazing at this wallpaper, when Linda came flying into the bedroom with her bathrobe on.

"Come on, Sandy! I've already taken out the snarls. You dry this side of my hair and I'll do the other."

Sandy immediately jumped off her bed to assist. The two sisters had a system and Sandy played her role well. This was not the first time Linda had asked for Sandy's assistance preparing for a date. Linda was a very pretty girl. She had an oval-shaped face; smooth, white skin; and gentle brown eyes. She had the perfect petite young woman's figure. She wore size five dresses that prominently emphasized her tiny waistline and slender hips. Sandy, even though she was seven years younger, could wear Linda's clothes; that's how petite Linda was.

Linda had beautiful long brown hair that flowed to her waist and she had to make sure it looked just perfect. In the late 1960s, perfect meant perfectly straight. This style demanded that not one wave exist anywhere in the hair. So, sitting on Linda's bed with both hair blowers on, the two proceeded to dry Linda's locks to straight perfection. After about forty-five minutes of the routine, Linda and Sandy turned off the blowers. Linda stood in front of the full-length mirror attached to the back of the bedroom door, and admired the results. She gave her sister a hug.

It may seem unusual that sisters with seven years between them were so close, but the bond had been cemented as soon as Mr. and Mrs. Lowenthal brought their new baby girl home from the hospital on a blustery winter's day. Seven-year-old Linda took one look at the new baby, bundled in thick, soft, woolen blankets, and instantly fell in love with her new baby sister. Baby Sandy became Linda's baby, and she was determined to teach her new sister everything she knew.

The lessons started young. One day, during Sandy's first summer, Linda had had enough of her six- month-old sister being able only to sit up in the playpen; it was now time for her to tackle the skill of walking. Linda made sure her mother was busy in the kitchen and then proceeded with baby Sandy's first walking lesson. She pulled Sandy from the playpen floor and made her stand up and hold on to the railing, because the baby was wobbly on her feet. Linda placed her hands over Sandy's, both now holding onto the playpen railing. However, the minute Linda let go of Sandy's hands her baby sister fell back down into the playpen. Linda, however, was determined. This ritual continued for almost an hour. Sandy was delirious with delight every time she fell back into the playpen. However, Linda was becoming discouraged about the prospect of her baby sister learning to walk that day. After all, Linda learned from her mother that Linda walked at six months. So, it made perfect sense that baby Sandy should be walking, too. Linda was ready to call it a day when she decided she would try it one more time, but just as she was pulling Sandy up from the playpen, her mother stepped into the living room and Linda had to push Sandy back down. She decided the walking lesson would have to continue another day.

There was a knock at the front door and Ginger, the family dog, who had a beautiful red coat and was a mix of Irish Setter and Cocker Spaniel, barked. Ginger was known to act more like a cat rather than a dog, because of her tenacious independence.

"Oh, Sandy, that must be Daniel. Quick, tell him I'll be right out. He hates waiting. I just have to put on my makeup and get dressed."

Sandy, from past experience, knew that for Linda to put on her makeup and find the right outfit to wear might take up to an hour, but she'd go out and face the slaughter alone.

When she entered the living room, Daniel was sitting on the couch, and in his usual anxious manner to get out of the house, asked Sandy in his typical, abrupt tone, "Is Linda ready?"

Sandy smirked and gave her usual response, "Almost," while she plopped down on the couch to watch television.

Daniel said under his breath, "Damn, what takes her so long!"

Mrs. Lowenthal came from the kitchen and seeing Daniel waiting, offered him something to eat. He politely refused, as his fingers tapped impatiently on his right thigh and his eyes snatched the time on his wristwatch. Mrs. Lowenthal sat down on one of the living room's overstuffed chairs and inquired, "Where are you taking Linda tonight?"

"Greek Town for dinner. We shouldn't be too late, Mrs. Lowenthal," assured Daniel, again sneaking a look at his wristwatch.

But Sandy knew better. Tonight was the night that Linda would be studying photography with Daniel and learning all about the different "angles of a camera." Though Sandy could only imagine the details of such complicated matters, it was enough to know Linda seemed to enjoy the "class." Just then, Linda came out of the bedroom, wearing her new dress and with her silken hair flowing, as she quickly walked toward her date. Daniel snapped to attention, stood up, and before you could count to three, he was helping her on with her coat and whisking her out the door. Mrs. Lowenthal yelled after them, "Have a good time. And be back no later than midnight!"

CHAPTER 5

Sandy's Secret

Sandy didn't especially like rising early for school. She enjoyed the comforts of her warm, cozy bed and the vivid dreams she often had. Knowing this, her father was sensitive to waking his daughter in a most gentle way—using bird-sounding kisses planted tenderly on her cheek. This morning, as her father reached her door on his way back to the kitchen, Sandy slowly roused, until she looked at the clock, "I only have twenty minutes before the tardy bell rings!" This time crunch propelled her into action.

This morning in particular, she hurried along washing, dressing, and eating breakfast, so she'd have enough time to tidy up the house a bit, since her friend Beth was coming over after school. Sandy looked around the spic-and-span house, beaming from ear to ear to see that yesterday's efforts were still paying off for today. She replaced a few of her mother's books on the bookshelf and now she was pleased and ready to go to school.

Today would be an exciting one, because a student council meeting was scheduled. Since Sandy was Student Council President, it meant that she'd be responsible for performing several interesting tasks, including presiding over the meeting. She enjoyed facilitating these meetings. It was Mr. Avery, the Principal of Tyler School, who taught her these leadership skills.

Mr. Avery had a slender build, and wire-rimmed glasses sat low on his nose with his strong-looking eyes focused out and above them. To Sandy, Mr. Avery always appeared to be doing several tasks at once. He was seen by all to be a commanding force in managing the day-to-day activities of the school. Children didn't revel in being sent to his office for misbehavior, for he was a noted stickler for making sure children obeyed school rules. He wanted Sandy to conduct the student council meeting properly, and called her to his office soon after the election.

"Sandy, congratulations on becoming Tyler School's Student Council President. It's an important responsibility. One, I'm sure, you'll handle well. One of your new responsibilities will be to preside over the meetings. So, I'm giving you this book, *Robert's Rules of Order.*"

Sandy took it from his hands, peered down at it, and gulped, thinking, *This is more complicated than I thought.*

"You must learn these rules, Sandy, regarding the proper etiquette for conducting a meeting."

Sandy looked up. "I'm going to read and then reread this book. I'm going to memorize every rule, I promise. I won't let you down, Mr. Avery."

"I'm sure you won't, Sandy. But I'll tell you what I'm going to do. I'm going to make my schedule available for all meetings, just in case you or the other students need my guidance."

Sandy felt relieved that Mr. Avery offered his support and felt more confident, knowing she could call on his expertise if she ran into difficulties. Student Council meetings were always held at lunch time and every class, starting from the third grade up, voted for its own representative. The officers, President, Vice-President, Secretary, and Treasurer, were elected in the fall and the whole school voted on these candidates. Sandy was proud that she'd been elected president and wanted to do her best.

An hour before each student council meeting, she met with her fellow officers to work together on creating an agenda, in order to conduct the business of the meeting. Today's outcome of the meeting produced:

> The Student Council Agenda of Tyler School
> January 18, 1967
> Progress to date on the Needy College Fund
> Canned Food Drive for the Poor
> Parents' Appreciation Day
> New Business

Sandy always started the meeting after everyone finished lunch. Today, the Student Council Treasurer, Dianne Phillips, reported: "Last week's successful bake sale allowed us to reach over $700!" The students started clapping upon hearing this news. The Treasurer continued, "I'm sure with five more bake sales left, we'll be able to reach our goal of $1,000." All the children felt proud about this and Sandy complimented everyone for working so hard.

Next on the agenda was the canned food drive. The Student Council Vice President, Roy McCardell, gave this report. He explained that every year the Student Council organized a canned food drive for the poor and this year it was planned for March, which was less than two months away. The students participated in a lively discussion about why this drive was so important and they hoped they could surpass last year's goal of donating more than 1,200 canned goods. A committee was chosen to help Roy plan and organize this event.

Sandy was excited for the next item on the agenda: Parents' Appreciation Day. She began explaining this item by reminding her fellow students what the Student Council had done the previous year. "Last year, all the fifth and sixth grade parents loved the pancake breakfast, but I was told by Mr. Avery that our budget for this year will be a lot less. So, as a Student Council body, we'll have to choose an event that will require less money. Does anyone have any ideas?"

Kathy Winer, a sixth grader, raised her hand. "Why don't we have a Parents' Appreciation Day by just honoring the mothers or fathers of the sixth grade class? After all, we'll be graduating in June."

Becky, another sixth grader, exclaimed, "That's a great idea! That'll bring the cost down by more than fifty percent!"

Kathy continued, "In May, it's Mother's Day. Why don't we do something just to honor the moms for Mother's Day this year? Say, a school luncheon with comedy skits?"

All the other student council members were feeling excited by the idea except Sandy. Sandy knew her mother would not attend such an event. Sandy was in a dilemma, but trying to save herself the embarrassment of not having her mother there, she blurted out, "Ladies always go first. Why don't we do it differently this time and honor the dads first, then next year we can have something special for the moms?"

Kathy spoke up. "Father's Day is toward the end of June, when school is already out for the year. And everyone knows moms have to come first!"

Sandy saw where this conversation was heading, and asked if there was any more discussion on the topic. Everyone loved the idea of a Mother's Day Luncheon, and when Sandy called for the council members to vote on it, every hand went up approvingly. Sandy was glad she was the President and only allowed to vote to break a tie, because in this case, she'd be the only one voting against a Mother's Day Luncheon.

After the meeting, Sandy returned to her classroom, where she reported on what had occurred. As she spoke about the planned Mother's Day Luncheon, she tried to present it in a positive manner. However, Sandy's good friends, Beth and Lynn, sensed Sandy pretending to be excited by the idea. Mrs. MacKenzie thanked her for the report and Sandy returned to her seat.

That afternoon, Mrs. MacKenzie started a new chapter in science, on the solar system. The students learned various scientific theories about how the universe was created. After they completed the assignment sheet that Mrs. MacKenzie had distributed, she said, "Class, I have something very exciting I want to discuss." The students all groaned. They knew when Mrs. MacKenzie started a sentence like this it meant more homework in some shape or form for them—and they were correct. Mrs. MacKenzie continued, "Tyler School's upper classmates, that is, the fifth and sixth graders, will be participating in the first-ever Science Fair, to be held on May 15th, which is approximately four months from now. This means you all get a chance to become scientists! Create a new invention, conduct an experiment, and intensively explore our universe!"

Some of the students truly were excited by the prospect. Sandy, loving science, was one of them, as was Lynn. However, Beth hated science and could have definitely thought of something more exciting, such as reading three extra novels and writing three extra book reports. Mrs. MacKenzie explained to the class they had two full weeks to think of their idea and write a page on it for her final approval. With that, the school day ended.

Books in hand, Sandy and Beth started walking to Sandy's house. The cold fresh air felt good to breathe after being in school all day. Sandy puckered up her mouth, making a small passageway to exhale a string of "smoke-circles," each one vaporizing as the next appeared.

"Sandy, what a great circle within a circle!"

"See, Beth, I've a little artistic talent."

The girls walked on, passing two little boys starting to build a snowman when one shouted, "You wanna help?" Without hesitation, Sandy and Beth turned around, threw their books down in the snow, and started assisting the boys roll the white, moist powder into a huge ball, for the base of the snowman. Within thirty minutes, the four of them stepped back to admire their creation.

"It's not bad," Beth said, "it's just missing its face."

Jimmy, the little six-year-old, said excitedly, "Look inside here!"

Beth peered into the bag, and the corners of her mouth turned up into a big smile. The little boy's mother had filled the bag with buttons, carrots, scarves, and M&Ms. Now, they had everything they needed for their snowman's face. With Beth directing, she had the little boys creating the eyes, nose, and mouth. They used the red and green M&Ms for the mouth, the carrot for the nose, and big black buttons for the eyes. Sandy put the red woolen scarf around the neck, and all four stepped back again, to admire their finished snowman.

Little Jimmy said, "Boy, that's the best snowman, ever! We're gonna build a fort next, can ya help?"

Beth turned to Sandy. "Come on, Sandy! Let's help 'em build it."

"I'd like to stay longer, but remember, Beth, we still have all that math to do."

"How can I forget? I was just trying to delay it as long as possible." The girls said good-bye to the little boys, wiped the snow off their books before picking them up, and headed to Sandy's.

"Ugh, I hate science!" protested Beth. "I've not the faintest idea of a project. What about you, Sandy?"

"Hey, let's not worry about that now. We've got two weeks to come up with an idea. And another four months before the project is due."

"Yeah, you're right, Sandy. Now let's just worry about getting tonight's homework done. Thanks for offering to help me with the fraction problems."

And before Beth spoke again, Sandy said, "Well, here we are."

"You live so close to the school. I didn't realize it."

"Cool, isn't it? Only seven houses away! But you know, when it's bad weather, my dad drives me to school."

"Wow," replied Beth. "Even when you live so close?"

"Yeah, it's on his way to work."

"Boy, you're lucky. I've got to walk five long blocks, even in the cold—and on wet, snowy days!"

They entered Sandy's house, and it was neat and tidy, just the way Sandy had left it in the morning. When they came in, Mrs. Lowenthal was reading a book. She stopped to greet the children and give them a snack of milk and cookies. When the girls were finished eating, Mrs. Lowenthal said it was nice to meet Sandy's new friend, and then excused herself, saying she had to go downstairs to do some ironing.

"Come on, Beth, let's go into my bedroom and work there."

Upon entering Sandy's bedroom, Beth exclaimed, "Wow, what cool colors! I love how you decorated this room, especially your wallpaper."

"Yep, isn't it cool? My sister and I redecorated it, a few years ago," Sandy said. The girls took out their math books to start tackling the forty fraction problems Mrs. MacKenzie had assigned. Beth was confused about finding the lowest common denominator within the more complicated problems. Sandy explained how she did it, and soon Beth understood it completely. After an hour Beth said, "Is it all right if I go into the kitchen and get more cookies?"

"Sure, Beth. Bring me a couple, too."

Beth returned to the kitchen and saw the bag of cookies on the table. As she approached it, a magazine lying there caught her eye. The magazine was entitled *Awake*. On its front cover, in big bold type, were the words:

PREPARE FOR ARMAGEDDON!

Beth had never heard of this word "Armageddon," and was fascinated with it. She took the cookie bag and the magazine back to Sandy's bedroom, where Sandy was still sitting on the bed, her back pressed up against the wall, legs stretched out, with her homework on her lap. She had only a few problems remaining, when Beth jumped back onto the bed. "Hey, look at this magazine I found on your kitchen table. What the heck is Armageddon?"

Sandy grabbed the magazine away from Beth, quickly putting it under her schoolbooks, and clearly embarrassed by Beth's finding it. She tried to change the subject, "Oh, it's just one of my mom's silly magazines. Come on, let's finish up, so we can play Monopoly."

Beth, seeing there was a dictionary nearby, reached for it. "As soon as I find out what the heck this word means." Beth quickly began looking up this strange word she had never seen before and found the dictionary's definition, reading it out loud to Sandy. "Armageddon—the scene of the final battle between the forces of good and evil, foretold in the New Testament. Wow!" said Beth. "This isn't something they teach at my Jewish Sunday school. Hey, I thought you were Jewish like me, and didn't believe in the New Testament?"

"I am," replied Sandy, as she pushed her glasses up on her nose, and her body stiffened. She jumped up from the bed and started pacing. And then, took a big breath, for now she was about to tell someone—for the first time—the truth about her mother. "Beth, remember how you hadn't told anybody about your mom's illness? Well, now before I tell you something, we must say Deep Talk over it." In less than a month, Sandy and Beth were entering into the secret pact for a second time. Beth immediately sprang from the bed, and like two soldiers standing erect, as if guarding a sacred monument, the two girls faced each other. They stared deeply into each others' eyes while locking onto each other's outstretched arms. They again counted in unison, and in a slow methodical tone, both girls pledged at exactly the same time, "One, two—Deep Talk."

Sandy, now breaking the hold, swallowed hard, lowered her eyes, and like a caged panther, paced the floor. Beth's eyes darted back and forth, following her. Abruptly, Sandy stopped, turned, and faced Beth. "Okay, you're the first person I'm telling in my whole life. Lynn doesn't even know about this—although she knows there's something strange about my mother." Sandy could feel her heart pounding and her stomach turning, for she was about to reveal the family secret. "My mom's not Jewish," she announced, and her face tightened.

"But I don't understand. I thought you said you're Jewish . . ."

"I am. My mom was Jewish, too, but—" and Sandy lowered her voice, "she changed religions and became a Jehovah's Witness, about five years ago."

"Never heard of it," answered Beth, gently, seeing how troubled her friend seemed over this issue.

"Believe me, I wish I hadn't either!" insisted Sandy, and she continued pacing the floor. "You've no idea how difficult it's been for me. I lie to all my friends about the real reason she doesn't come to services at the synagogue. And then her religion has some of the strangest ideas—like not even believing in celebrating birthdays, or holidays!"

"Doesn't believe in birthdays?" echoed back Beth, in disbelief.

"She didn't even come to my brother's Bar Mitzvah. When people asked where my mother was, I had to lie and say she was sick! And she never comes to my birthday parties either!" she added, with her face turning red.

"That's weird, Sandy. But why?"

"She calls it all paganism!"

"Paganism?" Beth asked, again reaching for the dictionary.

"Yeah, you better look that one up, too! But the worst thing is, she spends all her time reading her magazines and the Bible, and then goes knocking on people's doors, trying to convert them to believe like she does! No one else has the 'Truth about G-d', except the J.W.s!"

"Sandy, has she tried to convert you?"

"Of course, Beth. Everyone in this household! But thank goodness my dad finally put a stop to that!" Sandy exclaimed. "But my parents seem to be always arguing over something about religion."

What Sandy didn't share with Beth was lately, the fighting between her mother and father had become so intense, she'd use her pillow to cover her ears, drowning out her parents' shouting in order to fall asleep. And before falling asleep, she'd peer outside her small bedroom window, facing the backyard, where she saw the swing set her father had set up for her and her siblings when she was a small child. Sandy's eyes looked past Ginger's dog house. She gazed upward toward the sky and stared into the high heavens, where she imagined G-d spent most of the time, and she prayed. "Please, G-d, help my parents. Make them stop fighting with one another. Make them stop fighting about each other's religion. Isn't this your area? I know you can help me. G-d, please help this family."

Over the last several years, since Sandy's mother had adopted her new faith, and when Sandy returned from her Wednesday drama class, she saw either the rabbi from her synagogue or the elder from her mother's Kingdom Hall, talking to her parents. They would hold Bibles in their hands, reading from various scriptures. These sessions seemed to produce peace between Sandy's parents for a bit of time, and Sandy was most grateful that all was quiet on the battlefield.

During these periods of peace in the household, Sandy often heard her mother play at the family piano. Mrs. Lowenthal, although never having taken the piano lessons she'd wished for—because her parents were too poor to afford it when she was a child—was amazingly talented at the piano. She had taught herself how to play. More amazing was that when she heard a song she liked on the radio, she could sit down and play it. She had what is called a perfect ear. But predictably, somehow the truce was always broken between Sandy's parents. Resentments and anger seemed to slip back into the marriage, and religious differences always seemed to be at the core of the matter.

"Now I understand why you didn't seem so excited by the Mother's Day Luncheon event," said Beth, and her eyes revealed the tenderness she was feeling for her friend.

"Oh, for sure, going to that is against her religion, too," quipped Sandy. "Even if I begged her to come to the luncheon, told her the hours and hours we'd spent in getting ready for this day, she'd say something like . . . 'Why, every day is a special mother's day, in G-d's eyes, dear. I don't need a luncheon to tell me that'."

There was a long silence before Sandy spoke again. The bedroom window revealed dusk had arrived as its dim light slanted through the window, creating shadows in the room. Sandy finally broke the silence. "Beth, please don't tell anyone."

Beth replied, "Remember, it's already more than a promise. We've said Deep Talk over it."

And suddenly, the caged panther was free. For the first time since Sandy's mother had changed religions, Sandy felt tremendously unburdened, by sharing the family secret with Beth. Keeping the family secret had come at a price. Sandy had found it mentally and emotionally exhausting to constantly make sure she created the right stories and said the right things, so her friends and neighbors didn't find out the truth.

CHAPTER 6

Great Wealth

With spring fever in the air, the students in Mrs. MacKenzie's class desperately needed recess. Finally out on the playground, with the sun smiling and a gentle breeze tagging the children's faces, Lynn and Sandy initiated a game of tetherball. As they were playing, Lynn asked Sandy, "Do you wanna celebrate the second night of Passover with my family?" For the last two years, Sandy had done this with Lynn's family. Although Lynn did not know about Sandy's secret, she did know that Sandy's family had a small Passover celebration for the first night, but didn't have a Seder for the second night.

"I'd love to!" replied Sandy, as she punched the ball to the other side over Lynn's head.

"Great!" Lynn yelled, jumping up, trying to hit the ball as it sailed over her head. "We'll have fun, just like last year!"

"What about inviting Beth?"

"I think she'll be at her aunt's for Passover!"

"Well, did you ask her?" as she continued to play the game.

"No. I'm asking you to come, Sandy, not Beth," she snapped with her eyes glaring, as she leaped up and caught the ball.

"That's too bad; she'll miss out on the secret fun!"

Sandy cherished going to Lynn's house for the second night of Passover. It was always an exciting event. Lynn's mother, Mrs. Ernst, was a very attractive slender woman, with a full head of thick blond hair cropped just below chin length, and eyes, a sea-color blue. She always had a big celebration with many people attending, preparing traditional Jewish food, such as chicken soup, brisket, and tzimmes, a casserole dish made from carrots, sweet potatoes, and raisins, sweetened with honey.

But Sandy's favorite dish was Mrs. Ernst's gefilte fish, prepared with a ground whitefish mixture made into an oval shape, and served on a bed of lettuce with decorative carrots on top. Lynn never even had one bite of hers; she hated gefilte fish. Not wanting to hurt her mother's feelings, she'd secretly pass it under the table to Shawn, their white and brown mixed terrier dog, who immediately gulped it down.

Sandy thought Mrs. Ernst was one of the kindest women she'd ever met, and one of the wisest. Mrs. Ernst knew how to keep harmony in her house, even when the outside world could be filled with chaos. She kept a beautiful home, but for Passover especially, she made the house shine.

Mrs. Ernst also kept a magnificent flower garden. Her delicately scented roses were a much-discussed topic in the neighborhood. For Passover, she would cut some of her finest roses, along with other flowers, placing them in vases in beautiful bouquet-like arrangements throughout the house, making it smell sweet for the Passover holiday.

Over the last two weeks in Sandy's Hebrew class, they were learning about the holiday. She learned about the tradition for the adults to drink four glasses of wine throughout the Seder. Each glass of wine has special symbolic meaning associated with the holiday. Although the children usually drank grape juice, Mr. Ernst always poured a little wine for all of them without Mrs. Ernst knowing. The children who came to Lynn's house greatly anticipated this and knew how to "play the game," making sure the secret was between only Mr. Ernst and the children.

Mr. Ernst was a deeply religious man who practiced Orthodox Judaism and always kept the laws of the Sabbath. He went to synagogue services every Saturday, when most other Jewish men in Sandy's neighborhood were going to work. Mr. Ernst was short with a slight build, balding, and wore round, wire-rimmed glasses. When he walked, he stooped over a bit and had a slight limp. He had a thick and singsong Eastern European accent, and eyes that sparkled when he spoke. Mr. Ernst had a special exuberance for life, more so than any other person Sandy had ever met. He especially cherished children, and loved to share stories with them.

The Passover celebration brought out the best in Lynn's father. He started with, "My Kinder (Yiddish for children), I have in my hand," and he would hold the small book high, so everyone could see it, "The Hagaddah. Now, who knows what this Hebrew word means?"

Lynn yelled out, "Story."

Another child at the table said, "Freedom."

And Sandy yelled, "An old story."

"Very good, my Kinder, you all had the right idea, but the actual English translation is the retelling of a story. It is commanded in the Torah (Bible) that during this holiday we call Passover, we retell the story of our ancestors, when for four hundred years, we were slaves in ancient Egypt, when the pharaohs ruled, and how Moses, with the help from G-d, delivered us from bondage to freedom."

With this introduction, he began the service and started chanting in Hebrew from the Hagaddah. All present had a chance to read from the Hagaddah—some in English and some in Hebrew. A Seder at the Ernsts' could last for hours. Besides the Passover story that he was sharing with the children, he always took the time, in a gentle way, to explain to them that life for Jews in more recent times, as for Jews in ancient Egypt, was also most difficult.

"This time period," Mr. Ernst explained, "is known as the Holocaust. Mrs. Ernst and I are survivors of that most difficult time." And he took off his dinner jacket, rolled up his sleeve, and pointed to a tattooed number on his arm. "See this? I, like so many other Jews, became just a number. All other identity was taken away from me. I lost my home, my possessions and worst of all—my family. The Nazis took it all. But you know, my Kinder, they couldn't take my soul and my love for G-d. It was for these reasons that I could live on and be here tonight to celebrate yet another Passover. And when I look into your bright, young eyes, I see the future of our people with all of our hopes and dreams for a better tomorrow. I see all this in your eyes, my Kinder, and I truly know life is sweet."

Sandy was always deeply moved by what Mr. Ernst said at the Passover meal. As he continued the Seder reading and honored the traditions of the holiday, Sandy reflected upon the joyous way Mr. Ernst conducted his life, even after having experienced the cruelties of the Holocaust. And as she watched and listened to him, Sandy hoped she could live her life filled with appreciation for each moment, as did Mr. Ernst.

The next morning, unfortunately, the Jewish children still had to attend school. Sandy arrived at her classroom exhausted. Lynn, upon seeing Sandy said, "I almost didn't make it today. I'm so tired!"

"Me, too! Thanks, Lynn, for inviting me. I really enjoyed myself." Sandy sat down at her desk.

"I enjoyed it too, but it also makes me really upset," said Lynn, as she slumped into her wooden desk chair across from Lynn's.

"Because of your dad?" questioned Sandy.

"Yeah, when he talks about the Holocaust, I'm always reminded why my grandparents and cousins don't come to our Seders."

"But I thought Michael, Amy, and Carol were your cousins," said Sandy.

"Oh, no, they're our close neighbors, down the block. No, when my dad says he lost his whole family he means everyone—including my mother's side. I've no cousins, aunts, or uncles, just good friends like you, Sandy."

Sandy was taken aback by this revelation, and it made her feel heavy inside. It was difficult for her to imagine this reality, especially when she thought about how different her life would be without having her grandparents, aunts, uncles, and the cousins she adored playing with. She reached out her hand to Lynn's, across the aisle, "You'll always have me." Lynn grabbed Sandy's hand, and nodded her head in gratitude.

That school day dragged on and on for Lynn and Sandy. Finally the dismissal bell rang, and as the girls walked down the hall, Lynn said, "You know, Sandy, when you were over last night, I wanted to show you my science project, but forgot. Would you like to come see it today?"

"Sure!"

When they arrived at Lynn's house, she took Sandy downstairs to view the project. Sandy was quite impressed with it. Lynn had created a science experiment that demonstrated the process of photosynthesis. She had three poster boards put together in a u-shape. On each poster board was information pertaining to her experiment. On one poster board, she had written the basic scientific process of photosynthesis; on another, she demonstrated how her chosen plants had been given different amounts of time in the sun, and the effects of such time on her plants. On the third, she explained the symbiotic relationship existing between plants and humans. It stated, "Humans emit or breathe out carbon dioxide as a waste product, and breathe in oxygen to live. Plants do just the opposite; they absorb carbon dioxide, and emit oxygen as their waste."

Sandy had learned about this symbiotic relationship between plants and humans in science, but somehow seeing it in Lynn's project made her see it in a different light. She saw the balance, the need for each other, the give and take between humans and plants in a spiritual manner. She thought to herself, *It's a perfect relationship. It must have been made in heaven.*

"Lynn, this is a super project! Where did you get the idea?"

"Who else but the gardener in the family? My mother. After Mrs. MacKenzie gave us the assignment, I didn't know what to do. So for a week, every day after school, I'd go to the library and read books to figure something out, but I kept coming up blank. My mom, seeing I was troubled, suggested I study something about plants and how they grow. So I started to read up on this area and the word 'photosynthesis' came up. I had no idea what this meant, so I found out—and the photosynthesis project came to me."

"And you grew all these plants by yourself?"

"Yeah, my mom took me to a nursery and we got seeds, soil, and pots for the different plants. Then she showed me the proper technique of potting plants. We had a great time together!"

And suddenly Sandy realized why she so enjoyed coming to Lynn's house. *I love seeing Lynn and her mother together; they have a special bond that I wish I had with my mother. I can't remember the last time me and my mom had a great time together . . .* Sandy, if she was honest with herself, secretively wished that Mrs. Ernst could be her mother, too. Sandy thought, *I know for sure that Mrs. Ernst will be attending the special Mother's Day Luncheon, even if suddenly she came down with the worst illness in the world. Mrs. Ernst will be there for her daughter, enjoying the special day. My mom wouldn't, even if she was healthy enough to run a marathon.* This reality tugged at her insides. The painful ache refused to go away.

The wooden basement steps creaked under the pressure of Lynn's mother coming downstairs, carrying several elegant dresses draped over her arm. Mrs. Ernst exuded dignity, carrying herself with tremendous grace. Like her husband, she had a thick Eastern European accent, but unlike Mr. Ernst, in all the years Sandy knew Mrs. Ernst, she never talked to Lynn or Lynn's friends regarding her experiences in a concentration camp. It was only through Lynn's father that Lynn learned about how her mother suffered, during what Mr. Ernst described as "those dark days."

"Oh, my girls, I hope I'm not intruding," Mrs. Ernst said.

"Of course not, Mom. I was just showing Sandy my project that you helped me with."

"I just helped a little. You did all the work, my little one. Sandy, my Lynny worked real hard on her project, and I bet you did too."

"Yeah, only I needed a little help from my dad."

"So, *nu*, tell us what you did?" inquired Mrs. Ernst, as she hung the dresses on a nearby rack.

"I built a tornado," Sandy proudly announced, waving her hands in the air above her head to emphasize and demonstrate the idea.

"My goodness, a genius! You made a tornado!" Mrs. Ernst said, clearly impressed.

"Sandy, what made you think of doing that?" inquired Lynn.

"Tornados have always frightened me," declared Sandy.

"Me too," responded Lynn.

"And I don't care for them either!" stated Mrs. Ernst, clearing her throat and sitting down at the sewing machine. "So, what made you want to build one, Sandy?"

"I figured if I understood them better, perhaps I wouldn't be so frightened of them. So, with the help of my dad, I built a homemade tornado. You've got to come see it, Lynn!"

"What about tomorrow, after school?" asked Lynn.

"Great," replied Sandy.

"Sandy, do you remember the tornado last year that hit Lincoln Drug Store?" questioned Lynn.

"That was the scariest yet! I thought it was going to blow our house away!" exclaimed Sandy. "I was sitting on our living room couch on a Sunday afternoon watching TV, when I looked up and saw how dark and eerie it looked outside. The next thing I heard was the tornado sirens blasting, then my dad yelling for everyone to get down into the basement—fast! Then I heard a big noise, sounding like a locomotive—the tornado was roaring right down our street!"

"Thank goodness nobody got hurt; only property was destroyed. Property can always be replaced, but not our loved ones," said Mrs. Ernst, getting up from the sewing machine to give both Lynn and Sandy a warm embrace. "You know, girls," Lynn's mother continued, "the most precious gift we can give is our love and friendship. If you can go through life and hold up one hand and say I have these many friends, I mean true friends who will be with you in good and bad times, then you've found great wealth. So I wish for you both to have such great wealth in your life. Now, girls, please excuse me, I've some work to do." And she sat back down, turned the power on her electric sewing machine, and started the needed alternations on a customer's dress. Not only was Mrs. Ernst a fine gardener, she was an exceptional seamstress, and used this talent as her means of bringing in extra money to the household.

Sandy had never heard this definition of wealth before. It didn't seem to fit other people's definition of it. But Sandy liked this new definition right away and told herself she'd always remember it, vowing to achieve it in her lifetime.

CHAPTER 7

Science Fair

It was two days before Sandy's science project was due, and she was working diligently on it in the basement. Besides Tyler's Hill, the basement—which her father had transformed into a bright and cheery haven—represented Sandy's place of refuge, while she was at home. It was far from the hustle and bustle above her, with all the comings and goings of her two older teenage siblings.

She liked working on school projects and studying for exams here, but her favorite activity, knowing she was alone, was pretending to be an actress, performing on a grand stage in front of an audience. Sandy reveled in creating characters and stories, and playing to her imaginary audience, making sure to take the appropriate bows in acknowledgment of the thundering applause that always followed each of her performances.

Lately, however, Sandy was canceling all of her performances—at least until her science project was finished. And with only two days to go, there was still plenty of work. She needed to add the finishing touches on her tornado machine and complete her display boards. On one of the poster boards she planned to write: *TORNADOS: Facts Regarding One of Nature's Most Powerful and Destructive Forces*. On the other poster board, Sandy anticipated providing detailed information on safety tips to follow during a tornado. Once the poster boards were completed, she and her dad would take the machine with the posters to school, and display it at the Science Fair. Hundreds of visitors from the community were expected to attend the fair, not to mention all the family members coming, as well.

During the two-week display period, a designated time was planned when the judges would choose first, second, and third place winners. Sandy, who was quite competitive, was hoping to take first place.

She had found the design to her machine in a science book when she was researching material for the project at the local library. The diagram in the book looked like a three-foot wooden box kite. However, instead of paper, the four sides were made out of glass, with one-quarter-inch slits, so air could enter in a circular manner, both at the top and bottom. Before Sandy would demonstrate to her classmates how tornados are created, she wanted to do a test run one more time, in the privacy of her basement. However, this time she thought it would be more effective turning off the lights, to see if the newly installed electric light bulb in her machine was working properly. She turned her light bulb on and it worked.

She then proceeded to add the proper amount of cool water to the bottom of her tornado machine. This water was being held by a nine-inch pie pan. Underneath the pie pan was a one-burner heating element to heat the cool water, producing warm, moist air, that would rise through the machine's cooler air at the top, creating highly energized "storms", called "super cells." These cells give off energy called latent heat, creating an updraft. Then the tornado machine's open slits would allow for a wind shear effect to develop, or two layers of wind, creating fast wind entering near the top, and slower wind entering the bottom. This spins the updraft, which takes the shape of a funnel cloud and, *Voila*! A tornado is formed.

With the basement dark, except for the one light coming from the machine, Sandy saw her newly formed tornado moving faster and faster, creating a larger and larger funnel cloud inside the machine. This brought a big smile to Sandy's face, and a huge, excited scream—"I did it!"

Her excitement over the success of her project was momentarily disrupted when her father yelled down the stairs, "Sandy, the telephone is for you."

Before running upstairs, she took one more prideful look at her tornado, then pulled the plug to it, and went to answer the phone. "Hello? Slow down, Beth, I can't understand you."

On the other end of the telephone line was Beth, upset and crying, "I won't have enough time!"

"Time for what?" inquired Sandy.

"Oh, Sandy, it's been awful; my mom has been in and out of the hospital for the last month. I haven't told anyone, and I just couldn't get my science project done!" Beth said frantically.

"Mrs. MacKenzie will understand. You've had some problems," said Sandy, comforting her friend.

"Please, Sandy, I need your help!" pleaded Beth.

"But, Beth, the project is due in two days. It's impossible! I'm still working on my posters. Just tell Mrs. MacKenzie why you couldn't finish it. I'm sure she'll give you more time."

"You don't understand, Sandy. I need your help to buy time!" begged Beth.

"Buy time?" Sandy was puzzled by her friend's statement.

"For my mother!" shouted Beth.

"But I need more time to complete my project. I could take first place in the Science Fair. You should see my tornado go!" And her eyes lit up with excitement.

"Listen, Sandy, and try to understand. If my mother knew my project was going to be on display, she'd be so proud—it would help her to get out of the hospital faster, so she can come see it!" cried Beth.

Finally, Sandy was beginning to comprehend just how sick Beth's mother really was. "Okay, Beth. I'll be over in about a half hour." Sandy immediately dialed Lynn's number and before she heard the first ring, hung up. *What should I tell Lynn?* Sandy now faced a moral dilemma. *I really want to tell Lynn the truth about Mrs. Fine's illness. But I've already made a Deep Talk promise with Beth.* She redialed Lynn's number, and hearing her voice on the other end yelled, "Lynn, you gotta help me!"

"What's wrong, Sandy?"

"It's Beth. She can't complete her science project. She needs our help!"

"Oh, she does, does she?" Lynn seemed very uninterested in helping.

"Yeah, Lynn, she just called in a panic!"

"You know, Sandy, it seems that any time Beth calls you, you're ready to drop everything. Even your old best friend!"

"That's not true, Lynn!"

"Well, I think it is!" And in her anger, Lynn hung up on Sandy, and ran to her room. She accidentally ran into her mother in the hallway, carrying a dozen towels in her arms. The collision caused Mrs. Ernst to lose her balance, and the neatly folded towels tumbled out of her arms and scattered onto the floor. Lynn didn't even stop to apologize or help. She just headed straight to her bedroom and slammed the door. Mrs. Ernst, seeing her daughter was upset, didn't ask Lynn to help gather the towels. She was doing it herself, when she stopped to answer the phone, now ringing in the kitchen.

"Hello," answered Mrs. Ernst.

"This is Sandy, Mrs. Ernst. I really need to talk with Lynn!"

Mrs. Ernst heard the urgency in Sandy's voice. "All right, Sandy, dear, I'll see if she'll come to the phone."

Mrs. Ernst tapped gently on her daughter's bedroom door. "Lynny, dear, Sandy's on the phone for you."

"I don't wanna talk to her!"

Lynn's mother gently opened the door to her daughter's room and sat on the edge of Lynn's bed, near to where Lynn was sitting cross-legged, with her arms tightly folded against her chest.

"What's wrong, my Lynny?" Mrs. Ernst gently stroked Lynn's hair with her hand.

"It's Sandy! Ever since Beth moved here . . . Well, I feel left out." Mammoth tears ran down Lynn's cheeks. Mrs. Ernst hugged her daughter and wiped the tears from her daughter's eyes.

"I understand, dear. It's hard to share a best friend. But sometimes we have to, even when it hurts. Sandy sounds like she really needs to talk with you. Remember, we can only call ourselves a true friend, if we're there in the good and bad times."

Reluctantly, Lynn sulked off her bed and picked up the phone in the den. "Yeah, Sandy, what is it?"

"Lynn, you know how much your friendship means to me."

"Well, I'm not so sure anymore."

"I'd do anything for you. Now, you know that. But you're not having a problem right now. Beth is. She needs us now!"

"Is she sick?"

"Well, yeah, I mean sorta."

"Sandy, you're not making any sense. Either she's sick or she's not."

"She's sick all right. It's a phobia."

"What's that?"

"Lynn, it's this strange psychological condition that Beth caught. It's called a phobia."

"Well, can she take some medicine for it?"

"Well, it's not as easy as that. This condition is specifically known as 'Science-Project-Phobia,' or fear of starting and completing a science project."

It was times like these that Sandy was grateful to have older siblings, because she accidentally learned about the condition one afternoon when Linda was studying for her college psychology exam in the dining room. Linda had yelled out to Frank, their brother, since he was passing the bedroom, to get the book that was on her bed. Frank said he'd get it in a minute. Linda yelled back, "I need it, NOW!"

Frank shouted, "Then get it yourself! Your legs aren't broken!"

Sandy was coming up from the basement listening to the squabble between her siblings and hollered to Linda that she'd run and get it. Thank goodness she did. She picked up the book on Linda's bed entitled, *The Human Condition of Phobias*. Sandy, bringing the book to her sister, who was sitting at the dining room table with books and papers all around her inquired, "What the heck are phobias?" Linda, wanting to test her knowledge on the subject, since she would soon be given an exam on it, gave Sandy a lecture on the topic. Sandy now knew more about the psychological condition of phobias than she had intended, not realizing its import to her in the next month.

Lynn, upon hearing this news said, "I've never heard of this condition," and her entire attitude softened. "Poor, Beth, I'll try and help, if I can."

"And Lynn, when you see Beth, don't let her know that you know about her problem."

"Oh, I promise! I won't say a word to Beth about it."

Sandy hated deceiving Lynn. But a Deep Talk promise is not to be betrayed, under any circumstances. The consequences are too severe. Sandy assured Lynn that if the three of them worked hard tonight and after school for the next two days, it would be possible to help Beth finish.

That evening, Lynn and Sandy arrived at Beth's house at almost the same time. Before they entered, Sandy gave Lynn a big hug. "I knew I could count on you, Lynn."

"Remember what my mother said, 'A true friend is someone who will be with you in both good and bad times,' so, here I am." Sandy knocked on Beth's door.

Beth came to the front door and looked uneasy, but felt relieved that her friends were here to help. She immediately took them both downstairs. Sitting on Beth's ping-pong table was a volcano kit; it looked ominous to both Lynn and Sandy. Beth sensed their trepidation. "My Dad read the directions and thought it was pretty easy. He wanted to help me put this together, but he's been terribly busy with my . . ." Beth hesitated, and finally blurted out, "business matters."

Sandy was hoping that Beth would finally tell Lynn the real family crisis, but, seeing that Beth was not ready to share the secret, played along by saying, "Well, there's one way to find out."

She pulled the directions out of the box and started reading it out loud. The directions were very complete, and it gave a step-by-step diagram, depicting the volcano's schematics. After the volcano was built, it had to be painted and finally tested for its operational authenticity. The girls realized time was short.

Sandy had a plan and in a confident, matter-of-fact voice said, "Let's divide the work. Beth, you're the artist in the group; why don't you start on your poster boards?"

"I had a little different idea than poster boards," said Beth.

"Fine, then you work on that," said Sandy. "Lynn and I will build the volcano. After all, last summer, the two of us took first place in the sand castle contest!"

With everyone in agreement over their tasks, the girls plunged ahead. They continued late into the evening. Beth got her dad to agree to let her stay home from school pretending to be sick, in order to give her time to finish. And over the next two days, immediately after school, Sandy and Lynn came straight to Beth's, to continue the task. The volcano was now almost completed.

Beth, instead of using poster boards explaining the severe effects of active volcanoes, used her fine artistic abilities to create a mini clay replica of the city of Pompeii. This city, in 79 A.D., was destroyed by the destructive force of an active volcano. Beth created a flow of lava with miniature people being caught in the ravages of it, capturing the horror and shock on the faces of the city dwellers. Sandy and Lynn marveled at what Beth had accomplished in such a short time. They both had seen Beth's artwork in class and acknowledged her talent, but now they realized that Beth was truly a fine artist, at the age of only twelve. Sandy, holding up one of the clay figures exclaimed, "Beth, this is incredible!"

"Hey, can you give me some of your talent? I can barely draw a stick figure," said Lynn.

"Me? Look at that volcano sitting there." Beth walked straight to the ping-pong table, to admire it. "You've done a great job!" Beth beamed.

"Don't talk so fast, we have to test it, to see if it actually works!" exclaimed Sandy.

Sandy and Lynn added the correct amount of the necessary chemicals, as the directions stated, placing it inside the opening of the volcano, and within seconds the volcano "erupted," with great flows of "lava" spewing from its mouth.

"We did it!" yelled Lynn gleefully. And the three of them embraced and danced around the volcano, celebrating their joint accomplishment.

Stopping to catch her breath, Beth said, "Lynn, Sandy, thank you so much! I couldn't have done this without you!" She was filled with gratitude.

With Beth's project completed, and the girls totally exhausted from working so hard, Sandy called her dad to come pick her up and take Lynn home. As the girls were leaving, Sandy asked, "Beth, do you need help getting your project to school tomorrow?"

"Thank you, but my sister will help. I look forward to seeing both of your projects," said Beth. Suddenly Sandy felt her stomach tie up in knots, realizing her poster boards still were incomplete. She told herself, *Even though I'm exhausted; I've got to finish, even if it means no sleep!*

Arriving home, she rushed downstairs to work. Her eyelids barely open, she started the board explaining safety tips on how to survive a tornado. An hour's time went by and she realized, *Gee, I'm not doing my best work. I'm just so tired,* and sighed in frustration. *I know what to do. I'll close my eyes for fifteen minutes to get some rest, and then start again.* However, when her eyes opened, it was morning. Sandy woke up groggy, with her face lying on the poster board. She shielded her eyes with her hands from the bright basement lights that had remained on, after she unintentionally fell asleep. She slowly picked up her head upon hearing the sounds of her father's footsteps coming downstairs. Sandy thought to herself, *How stupid can I be! I can't believe I fell asleep!*

Mr. Lowenthal saw the bloodshot eyes of his daughter and the strain on her face. "You must have worked until the wee hours of the morning. I'm sure the posters look great."

"No, Dad, I tried to finish but I fell asleep. Now, I'll never have a chance to win the Science Fair!" moaned Sandy.

"Sure you will, dear, your tornado machine is a great achievement in itself. I bet the judges will love it!" Sandy's dad said trying to reassure her.

"You really think so?" replied Sandy as she gazed at her machine.

"Of course I do," insisted Mr. Lowenthal. "Come on, dear, help me get it into the station wagon, and we'll take it to school."

Sandy, feeling better, helped her dad. When they arrived at Tyler School, there was a large sign in the lobby that read:

ALL SCIENCE EXHIBITORS REPORT TO THE GYMNASIUM.

Sandy and Mr. Lowenthal entered the gym to find it ablaze with activity: all the children, with the assistance of their parents, were setting up their projects. Sandy and Mr. Lowenthal found the perfect spot in which to place the tornado machine. Then, Mr. Lowenthal suggested they walk around to see some of the other projects. Sandy liked this idea and she and her father strolled hand-in-hand, surveying the other children's works. As they walked, Sandy started sensing that sinking feeling in the pit of her stomach, as she saw that most of the children had impressive display boards, further describing their project. Mr. Lowenthal sensed his daughter's nervousness. "Sandy, your project is very good, honest, you'll see. But, dear, the main reason for doing it was to learn something you didn't know before."

"Well, I can honestly say I know a hundred times more about tornados than I did four months ago."

"Then, that's all there is to say. Winning or losing the science contest is not the point," said Mr. Lowenthal, as he looked into his daughter's eyes.

"I understand," said Sandy, squeezing her father's hand as they continued through the gym.

All the fifth and sixth grade children eagerly anticipated the following week, because on Friday evening the school was having a formal awards presentation, for the winners of the Science Fair. Sandy was nervous. Even though she remembered the conversation she had had with her father about winning the science contest, she still wanted to win. If she came in first, second, or third place tonight, then she and her tornado machine would be off to the State competition, where children had a chance to win incredible prizes—even a chance to win a free trip for her and her family to Disneyland. The trip to Disneyland was what Sandy really wanted.

Sandy arrived with her father to the awards presentation to see all her friends with their parents. She was especially happy to find Beth present, with both her parents and two sisters. She walked over to Beth and, seeing an empty chair next to her, sat down and whispered in her ear, "Your mom made it!"

Beth whispered back, "She just got out of the hospital today. She's real weak, but she said she wouldn't miss this for the world."

The girls continued talking quietly, so Beth's mom couldn't overhear the conversation, "That's great," replied Sandy, seeing how happy her friend looked.

"When I took her to see my project, she was so thrilled! Sandy, I can never thank you and Lynn enough for helping me."

The girls' conversation was interrupted when Mr. Avery, the principal of Tyler School, came to the podium, dressed in a handsome navy blue suit and red tie, and asked everyone to please take their seats and quiet down, so he could begin the awards presentation. Children and parents stopped ambling around the gymnasium to find a place to sit. Mr. Avery began his remarks. "I'm proud of each and every one of you for working so diligently and producing excellent science projects. As you know, this is the first time Tyler School has ever had its students enter such a contest. There will be three official winners of the Science Fair, third place, second place, and our first place winner. All finalists will have the honor of representing Tyler School in early June at the State Science Fair held in our capital of Lansing.

In my mind, everyone is a winner tonight! I wish I had ribbons for each and every one of you. However, I must follow the rules of the contest and present these honors to our three finalists. The judges, representing the fourth grade teachers, to ensure impartiality and fairness, informed me they had a most difficult time selecting the winners."

Sandy, as she listened to Mr. Avery, was getting jittery. Her heart began pounding and her palms started to feel wet and clammy. Deep down, she wanted to win. In her mind she was going for the big trip to Disneyland. She secretly wanted to hear Mr. Avery call out her name.

The principal continued, "Now, I will announce their decision: The third place winner is Catherine Knoll, for her creation of a record on her self-made phonograph. The second place winner is Thomas Levy, for his construction of a sound wave machine, and his ideas for reducing sound pollution in the environment. And the distinction of Tyler School's First Place Winner goes to sixth grader Miss Beth Fine, for her construction of an active volcano, and her clay model depiction of the city of Pompeii, which was destroyed by the forces of an active volcano known as Mount Vesuvius."

Sandy squeezed Beth's hand. Beth jumped up in delight, when she heard Mr. Avery call her name. Before walking to the stage, she knelt down to her mother, who gave her a warm embrace. When Beth was receiving her award, Sandy turned around to look at Beth's mother. She had tears running from her eyes as she clapped proudly for her daughter. And suddenly, Sandy felt moisture, too, coming from her own eyes—they were tears of joy, as she glanced back up to her friend, now holding her trophy and acknowledging the audience's recognition of her award by the loud applause.

That evening, though Sandy did not take first place for her tornado machine, she came closer to understanding there were more important things than winning awards. Sandy may not have realized the importance of the moment she helped to create for Beth's family. A moment that would be meaningful to each and every member of the Fines for a lifetime—but she could feel and embrace the joy, joy that continued to bring a steady flow of tears to her eyes.

CHAPTER 8

Mother's Day Luncheon

Like a bull entering the arena, Sandy charged into the small, brightly lit bathroom and pleaded, "Mom, you've got to come!" Mrs. Lowenthal was facedown in the sink, cleansing the previous night's cold cream off her face. Mrs. Lowenthal paid special attention to the care of her complexion. Her morning ritual could easily take up to forty-five minutes or more. But the effort paid off. She probably had the most luminous and softest complexion one was bound to see in the Midwest.

"I'm sorry, dear. I can't," her mother replied in a matter-of-fact tone, as she gazed into the mirror and applied her daytime moisturizer. "Remember, Sandy, if you want a young looking face, you have to moisturize your skin." Mrs. Lowenthal was now admiring hers in the mirror. "See, dear, there's not a wrinkle on my face."

Sandy barked back, "I don't care about wrinkles! I care about you coming to the luncheon!"

"Sandy, it's against my moral principles," Mrs. Lowenthal replied calmly, as she was rinsing out the sink.

"But, I'm the Student Council President. You'll miss my speech!" Sandy reproached her, tearfully. "For heaven's sake, Mom, I'm not asking you to steal, cheat, or lie for me! Only to come tomorrow to my school's Mother's Day Luncheon! How wrong can that be?"

"You know Jehovah's Witnesses don't celebrate pagan beliefs," replied Mrs. Lowenthal, as she closed the lid on the Ponds jar, picked up her Bible, and went to sit down in the living room to read it. Sandy, like a wound-up top, followed her mom out of the bathroom and into the living room, where she continued her plea. "I'll be the only kid without their mom! Please, can't you make this one exception?"

"Now that would be lying to G-d, Sandy. And I want to live forever in G-d's kingdom," she said proudly. "And I'd like it for you, too. Why don't you come with me to the Kingdom Hall this evening?"

"I wouldn't be caught dead going there," hissed Sandy. "You're never gonna convert me! I just wanna live with a normal mother, but I can't!" shouted Sandy. "The only thing that you care about is not getting wrinkles and converting more people to your stupid religion! You only care about yourself. You don't care about me . . . what I need! Well, I hope one day you'll find yourself looking in the mirror counting a thousand wrinkles on your face!"

Sandy stormed out of the living room and into her bedroom, slamming the door behind her, which accidentally caused the hand mirror lying precariously on the edge of the dresser to fall. Her hopes of her mother changing her mind were just as shattered as the now-broken hand mirror lying scattered on the carpeted bedroom floor. Sandy, oblivious to the accident, collapsed onto her bed. She hadn't even noticed her sister, Linda, on the opposite side of the room, sitting on her twin bed doing homework.

Linda obviously noticed the accident, but didn't say a word about it. Instead she asked, "Hey, can big sisters come?" obviously having overheard the commotion and wanting to help her little sister. Linda came over to Sandy and sat on the edge of her bed, reaching out to hold her sister's trembling hand.

Sandy fell into Linda's arms sobbing, and Linda quietly stroked her little sister's hair soothingly. After Sandy's tears subsided, she said, "With all the mothers in the world out there, we've got to get this one!"

Sandy tossed and turned in her bed. Sleep eluded her as her mind wrestled with her situation. *I'm the only girl on the planet with a mother not wanting to be at the Mother's Day Luncheon. Me, her own daughter, has worked on it for hours, planning it, then rehearsing it and rehearsing again. For what? She won't even hear my speech!* She was already feeling the embarrassment as she imagined herself walking into the school without her mother and having everyone ask, "Hey, Sandy, where's your mom?" Then she knew what she had to do. *I'll lie. But what lie to tell?*

She thought about a dozen or so scenarios. But the ones that sounded most convincing were the very ones that would also have kept Sandy away from the special event, like a fabricated car accident, sudden major illness, or kidnapping. She'd hardly be at the luncheon if her mother had been kidnapped! Or would she? Her stomach started to tighten and her breathing became more rapid as she thought about this last scenario. Sandy had to be truthful to herself, and that truth meant, as hard as it was to admit, life in the Lowenthal household promised more happiness and peace if her mother, somehow, magically disappeared.

In the stillness of their bedroom, Sandy heard her sister's slow, easy breathing as Linda slept, with the moonlight sneaking through the window and seemingly kissing her pretty face. This had a calming effect on Sandy, as she gazed across the room at her sister and knew she could always depend on Linda to be there for her.

Sandy's anxiousness subsided, and her mind saw the problem in a different light. *Perhaps with all the excitement, speeches, and comedy skits nobody will notice that my mom isn't at the Luncheon.* That is what she prayed for—and then she'd be able to avoid lying.

Sandy arrived early to school that morning in order to participate in the final dress rehearsal. When she arrived, she was truly amazed to see that the usually stuffy, drab looking gymnasium had been transformed into an attractive banquet hall. The art teacher, Mrs. Tanner, had selected the best of students' artwork, and had each piece artistically placed on all the walls. A sweet smell came from the assorted spring flowers sitting in the center of each table, dressed in beautiful white linen. The rehearsal went perfectly and just as they were finishing, the mothers started entering.

Name tags, in alphabetical order, were put by every place setting. It was decided that the children be placed next to their mothers. Sandy, as Student Council President, was seated at the head table, with the principal, Mr. Avery. The other student council officers, along with their mothers, were also placed at the head table.

Beth arrived alone; she sat down in front of her name tag, and started twisting her curls with her index finger. When Sandy spotted her sitting unaccompanied, twisting her curls, Sandy knew that meant her friend was nervous. She approached Beth and whispered in her ear, "Is your mom all right?"

Beth shook her head no. "My mom is feeling really weak today."

The girls' teacher, Mrs. MacKenzie, looking lovely in a flower print cotton dress, overheard them talking. "I'm sorry your mother won't be here today, Beth. She'll be missing a fun filled event. Sandy, I'm looking forward to meeting your mom; I haven't met her yet. In fact, I don't think I've seen her at any of the functions."

Sandy, stammering, replied, "Well, uh, not today. She . . ." Sandy felt like a fish out of water, groping for some air.

Beth, seeing her friend was in trouble, blurted out, "It looks like Sandy's mother is suffering from the same flu that my mother is."

Sandy, grateful for Beth's support in helping her out of the awkward moment, regained her composure and confirmed the feigned illness of her mother. "It's really quite a bad flu, Mrs. MacKenzie. It just seemed to come out of nowhere. I hope we don't get it!"

Once everyone was settled, Mr. Avery began. "We are proud to have the sixth grade girls and boys honor their mothers today at Tyler School's First Mother's Day Luncheon. I would like to introduce our first speaker, President of Student Council, Sandy Lowenthal." With the audience clapping as Sandy went to the podium, she nervously put her note cards on the lectern and began her speech.

"Good morning to all the mothers, with their sons and daughters. We are delighted that so many of you could attend our First Mother's Day Luncheon. This event is to let all the mothers know that your children are all standing up here today through me, as their representative, to say thank you for being mom. Thank you for doing all that you do to help us be who we are. We may not always stop to tell you how much you mean to us, so we come together today to say jointly: Thanks, Moms, for being there!"

As she finished, she saw the smiles on the moms' and children's faces and she knew her speech was well received. Then she saw her friend, Lynn, in the audience sitting with her mom and wished today Mrs. Ernst could have been her mother, too. After the clapping stopped, Sandy continued. "Moms, you are in for a special treat today, because we have great comedy skits prepared for you before your lunch is served."

The comedy skits went on without a hitch and Sandy, judging by the amount of roaring laughter booming through the gymnasium, knew that everyone was really enjoying it. The skit that evoked the most laughter was entitled, "Little Nephew Tommy." Sixth graders Carolyn and Sam were playing the roles of Husband and Wife, when the Wife gets a frantic call from her sister, being played by twelve-year-old Sally, pleading for the Wife to watch her two-year-old son, Tommy, for the day because she was suddenly called into work at the hospital. Tommy was being played by Glenn, the class clown from Mrs. MacKenzie's class. The Wife agrees in spite of the Husband's reluctance.

"Little Nephew Tommy"

WIFE	Rick, we must help my sister!
HUSBAND	But, Sharon, we don't know anything about kids!
WIFE	For heaven's sake, Rick, little Tommy is our nephew. We'll be able to handle it.
	(Knock at the door)
SISTER	I can't thank you enough! Now, here are Tommy's things. *(Hands bag to Wife)* You won't have to worry, there're plenty of diapers.
HUSBAND	Diapers? But, I thought little Tommy was potty trained!
SISTER	*(Laughs)* I wish! *(Runs out the door)*

HUSBAND	*(Anxiously calling out the door)* When will you be back?
	(No answer)
WIFE	Well, this is swell, Tommy, to have you with us today. Your Uncle and I have great plans! We're going to take you to the park, try out the swings and the slide. How does that sound?
TOMMY	Go, park?
HUSBAND	Boy, is my nephew smart! He really knows what we're talking about!
TOMMY	*(Starts crying)* Mommy. Me want Mommy!
WIFE	Sure, mommy will be back later! But now we're going to the park.
TOMMY	*(Kicks the table, vase falls and breaks, runs around the room, screaming. . .)* Me want Mommy!
WIFE	*(Sits on the floor)* Tommy, look at these toy blocks. These are great fun.
TOMMY	*(Sits down to play with the blocks and stops his tantrum)*
WIFE	*(Playing with blocks)* These blocks are fun, Tommy! See, I told you you would like this. *(To husband)* Dear, come join in.
HUSBAND	*(Sits down to play with the blocks, to Wife)* Boy, I'm glad you thought of the blocks! That was a rough start! Great job, Tommy.
	(Tommy is now stacking the blocks up high.)
HUSBAND	Here, I'll help you. Did your mother teach you how to play with blocks?
TOMMY	*(Starts throwing the blocks and screaming . . .)* Me want Mommy! Me want Mommy!
WIFE	Rick, why did you mention that word?
TOMMY	*(Goes into another tantrum)* Me want Mommy! Me want Mommy!

HUSBAND	How was I supposed to know?
WIFE	Don't you know anything about kids?
TOMMY	Me want Mommy! (*Kicks his uncle in the shin*)
HUSBAND	(*Holding his leg in pain*) Sharon, do something about this!
TOMMY	Me want Mommy! Me want Mommy!

(End of skit)

When the luncheon was over, she watched the moms hugging their children with delight, remembering that her mom was at home, and most likely reading the Bible. Or even worse, she thought, *My mother is going around some neighborhood, knocking on people's doors, trying to convert them to her religion, when she should have been here!* She felt her face flush with anger.

Sandy thought she deserved an "A" in pretending to enjoy herself. *Those Monday night acting classes are really paying off,* she said to herself. Her energy depleted, she was ready to go home, but realized she had another two hours, before school was over. When she returned to her classroom, it seemed unbearably stuffy, even though all the windows were open and the classroom flag was swaying from the breeze flowing in. Beth was waiting for her. "Sandy, I think it's a day when you may want to come to my house after school and just watch the tadpoles swim."

"Yeah, I'd like that." Sandy slumped slowly into her classroom seat, laying her head down and closing her eyes.

Before long the girls were sitting on the grass in Beth's backyard, on this beautiful spring day, the sun gracing their bodies with gentle warmth, through the open patches between tree branches. An endless array of butterflies flew near the newly blossomed sunflowers and then to the pond, looking as if they were drinking hungrily to quench their thirst. The girls sat under the willow tree, near to the pond's edge, each staring into it, lost in their own thoughts.

Sandy's eyes caught the activity of the tadpoles as they swam continuously around and around rocks at the bottom of the pond. She noticed that some of the tadpoles' tails were beginning to change into legs, as they became frogs, following the course of nature's plan. As she continued peering down at them, she caught her own reflection in the water and stared at it. As of today, she saw no changes in her body, of the kind she was told to expect from last year's fifth grade movie on puberty. And she was thankful. Sandy wasn't in a hurry to grow up. She wasn't eager for those changes to occur, and secretly hoped that Mother Nature might forget about bringing them to her. But according to that movie, this change is inevitable. It's a rite of passage into womanhood, as explained in the film, and it was best to be prepared for it. But she wondered if anybody was really ready for changes? *Even if you don't want them*, she thought, *change has its own way of just showing up in your face, and saying, I'm here. Deal with me.*

As the sun was beginning to hide for the day and the air grew chilly, Beth suggested they go inside, not knowing that her father and her sisters had just returned from the hospital. Beth and Sandy walked into the den, where Beth's family sat. Sandy saw their sullen faces, and felt a great sadness, like a big, black cloud of smoke hovering around Beth's family members. Beth knew immediately that something was terribly wrong.

"Where's Mom?"

Mr. Fine met his daughter's eyes and getting up from the couch, reached out to Beth, to lovingly embrace her. He choked back tears. "Your mother's suffering has ended; she's with G-d now."

Beth buried her head into her father's chest, and Sandy heard gut-wrenching sobs pouring out of her friend.

Sandy wanted to run to Beth and comfort her, but knew it was not the time. It was the time for Beth's family to be alone, and she quietly opened the front door and slipped out. Sandy walked home, hardly believing what she had just heard. She kept thinking over and over, *How could this have happened? This just isn't fair.* She just couldn't fully comprehend that Beth's mother was no longer living.

When Sandy entered her house, Linda was sitting on the couch watching television. She took one look at her sister and knew something was dreadfully wrong.

"Sandy, what happened?"

Sandy ran into her bedroom, her sister on her heels. "Was the Mother's Day Luncheon that awful?" Linda asked.

Sandy, who had thrown herself onto her bed, sat up and managed to say, "It's Beth's mother—she died today."

Linda was shocked by the news, but seeing how upset Sandy was, did not ask any questions, just held her little sister for the longest time. The bedroom telephone rang. Linda answered, fully prepared to tell whomever it was to call back later. She picked up the phone and heard the voice on the other end. "Wait one minute, she's right here. It's for you Sandy; it's Beth."

"Sandy, can you tell Mrs. MacKenzie I won't be at school for the rest of this week? After the funeral, we'll be sitting Shivah." Sandy had learned in Sunday school about her faith's tradition of sitting Shivah, or paying respects at the deceased person's home, for up to seven days. She was taught that prayers are recited and food is brought, so the family need not concern themselves with meal preparation, but most importantly, her Hebrew teacher said, "We go to the Shivah House to give support, love, and kindness; we especially attend so the family is not alone in their grief."

"Can you bring me all my homework assignments and books?" asked Beth, twisting her curls.

"Sure, Beth. I'll get everything for you. Don't worry about it."

There was a long pause and Beth's voice cracked, when she asked her friend the next question, "Sandy, will you come to the funeral tomorrow?"

"I'll be there, Beth," replied Sandy sorrowfully, and as she hung up the receiver on the pink, princess style phone, she wondered what to expect. She had never been to a funeral, and it made her uneasy. She thought, *What can I say to Beth? What should I say? How can I make Beth's pain go away? How can I help her to forget?* She recalled the words she heard Beth's father say, "Your mother's suffering has ended; she's with G-d now."

Sandy wondered, *How did Mrs. Fine get to G-d so quickly? Is this really what happens?* Sandy was taught in Hebrew school that we're more than flesh and blood. She was taught that G-d gives everyone a soul and it lives, even after the body does not. But Sandy felt confused about this immortal soul, this spirit within her body. And as her mind conjured images of her own spirit, she felt her heart within her chest, beating faster and faster until her thoughts were finally disrupted by her sister.

"So, what did Beth say?"

"She wanted to know if I'll be at the funeral tomorrow."

The next day, Sandy's father accompanied her to the funeral. When Sandy saw her grief-stricken friend at the cemetery, she wanted to run to her, tell her she would get through this. However, it was impossible for Sandy to approach Beth, because so many of her relatives crowded around her. After the funeral, Mr. Lowenthal and Sandy went to Beth's house to sit Shivah.

When they arrived, it was difficult for Mr. Lowenthal to find a parking place, because cars were lined up and down the block. Before they finally found a space three blocks from the house, Mr. Lowenthal said, "You've been a wonderful friend to Beth. She needs you now, more than ever." Sandy nodded her head in agreement.

By the number of parked cars, Sandy knew many people were at Beth's house. Walking arm and arm, Sandy and her father approached the Shivah house. As they walked on this clear spring day, she looked up and noticed robins flying from treetop to treetop. The sky looked silky smooth, with wisps of white ribbon running through it. She paused, closed her eyes, and caught the warmth of the sunrays before climbing the front porch. On it, Sandy saw a pitcher of water, a bowl, and towel, not understanding their purpose until she watched her father.

"Sandy, dear, it's customary in our faith when we enter a house of mourning returning from the cemetery, that we wash our hands before entering." Silently, Sandy, too, performed the ritual and then they entered.

Indeed, it looked to Sandy as if more than a hundred people were crammed full into the house, paying their respects. In the hallway was a burning candle, in memory of Beth's mother. As Sandy looked for Beth among the many faces, she heard snippets of their conversations, even though they were speaking in quiet voices.

"Before her illness, she was the most devoted mother that I've ever seen," said one guest.

Another shook her head in agreement and whispered, "It'll be the toughest on the youngest."

Sandy knew they were talking about her friend, as she continued searching for Beth. Sandy walked through the kitchen, living room, and at last found Beth in the family room, again surrounded by dozens of people. A woman, maybe Beth's aunt, Sandy thought, was sitting next to Beth on the couch. The woman got up and walked toward the kitchen. Sandy seized the opportunity to wiggle her way through the crowd and finally sat next to Beth. As they embraced, Sandy felt her friend's tenseness. Now, Sandy, finally in close proximity to Beth, noticed how ashen her face looked and how red and puffy her eyes were from crying.

Beth's voice seemed almost inaudible to Sandy when she spoke, "Sandy, I'm so glad to see you. I wasn't sure if you could miss school to come." Without giving Sandy time to respond, Beth continued, "I really need a breather from all my relatives. Come with me."

Taking Sandy by the hand, they weaved through clusters of relatives and friends until the girls were upstairs in Beth's bedroom, where she quickly closed the door. Beth took an envelope from underneath her pillow and the two girls settled down, cross-legged on the pink, carpeted floor.

"Look, this is a letter from my Mom, before she died. I haven't read it to anyone yet. But I want you to hear it. It's important to me. Is that okay?"

Sandy was both moved and amazed at Beth's strength at a time like this. The fact that her friend was sharing such a personal letter with her touched her deeply, and she quietly answered, "Sure."

And before Beth began, the room filled with silence. Sandy closed her eyes. She thought she could hear the air currents moving about her, and then she heard Beth remove the letter from the envelope. The sounds were crisp and purposeful. Beth started reading.

May 29, 1967

My dear little girl, I know how sad you must feel right now, knowing I can't give you a kiss every night and tuck you in bed, even though I know you think you're getting too old to be tucked in. It's all right for you to be angry with me for not being there. I'm angry too, that I won't be there to see my little girl graduate this year from elementary school, and all the graduations yet to come.

I'm sorry I won't be there for your first date, or to dry your tears with your first heartbreak. Please forgive me. However, I do believe I've made it this far because of you. Beth, you have given me such strength to live.

My dear, you are such a smart, creative young girl. Whatever you pursue in life, I know you will do it well. I won't worry about you, because I see you know how to pick good friends. And I know your father and sisters will be there for you.

Beth, now you must use your strength to live on through this difficult time and grow into a young woman that I'd be so proud of.

Now, my dear one, I want to give you a special gift to remember me: this diamond necklace I wore when I married your father twenty-five years ago. Perhaps you'll wear it at your wedding. Remember, Beth, I'll be with you in spirit, always.

Your loving mother.

As Beth read, Sandy couldn't stop her eyes from raining. When she gazed up at Beth, she saw one tear drop fall silently onto the letter, as if it were a kiss. After Beth finished, Sandy had no words to say to her friend. She could only embrace her. And as she held her friend, Sandy thought of her own mother. It was only yesterday at the Luncheon when she wished to have another mother, one who would have joyfully attended the special school event. Now she just felt relief, knowing her mom would still be alive when she returned home.

CHAPTER 9

Miller's Haunted House

Mary Miller was one of the few Catholic children in Mrs. MacKenzie's class. Mary was a quiet, shy, and reserved child, and quite poor. Her brown hair was often pulled back in a ponytail, emphasizing her seemingly sad, brown eyes. Her parents made their living by maintaining the only local farm in the area. The Miller farm could not compete with the larger, more modern farms of the time, however. Mary was one of ten children. She often came to school wearing worn out clothes, looking as if they were too large for her body. She stood in sharp contrast to her fellow classmates, who came from primarily white, Jewish, middle-income families, as well as several from middle-class Protestant families—most of whom could afford to dress in the latest fashions. Although the other children did not tease Mary, nor were they mean to her, they did not readily include her in their play at recess time; she was often found playing alone on the swings.

Mary Miller hesitantly approached Sandy in class, during the week Sandy was attending Shivah at Beth's. At the pencil sharpener in the back of the room, Mary said, "Sandy, my mother has made some baked goods for the Fine family. Do you think you could come to my house today, to take it to Beth's?"

"It's perfectly okay for you to bring it to her," Sandy replied, as she finished sharpening her pencil. "I'm sure she'd be happy to see you."

"Oh, I couldn't. But you're Beth's closest friend."

"Okay. I'll take it over to the family," agreed Sandy.

That day after school, Sandy started to walk home to Mary's house with her, when Mary said, "Don't you wanna' go home first, to ask your mother if you can come over?"

"That's okay, I'll call from your house."

Mary, looking embarrassed, responded quietly as she studied the toes of her shoes. "We don't have a phone."

Sandy hid her surprise. "Then I'll just run home to tell my mom, and I'll be right back." Within six minutes, Sandy and Mary were headed toward the Miller farm. Though Mary's house was about a mile from school, she knew short cuts through the small crop of woods still remaining in the community after the new housing developments were built, and Sandy followed her lead.

After ten minutes, Sandy suddenly stopped. "What wrong?" Mary asked.

"If we continue down this path, we'll come to Miller's Haunted House," Sandy replied, with her eyes wide open, and locked onto the path.

The shyness that Mary exhibited in class suddenly disappeared as she replied confidently, "Well, it depends on what you mean by haunted. It's just the spirit of my great-grandmother, waiting for her husband to return."

Sandy was completely baffled by Mary's strange and assertive response. Continuing down the path, Sandy said, "Your great-grandmother's spirit? You really don't believe in all that stuff, do you?"

Mary did not answer Sandy's question; instead, she replied, "Listen to this story.

"The year was 1863. The Civil War had been going on for two years. Michigan was calling upon more young men to join the Union's army—for they desperately needed soldiers. Together, my great-grandparents farmed this land, and were raising a family of ten children, like my family today. The family stories that were passed down to my father, and now to us include one about the special love they had that few marriages ever achieve.

"The story goes that my great-grandmother begged her beloved husband not to enlist, because she had just become pregnant, and needed him during this time. She asked him to wait until after the birth. He explained to her that he had a duty to his family, but he also had a duty to honor and his country. He could not wait—the Army's reserves were critically low, it was a turning point in the war, and he felt he could help make a difference. He decided by week's end he would enlist. However, he promised her if she lit a candle in the window every night for him, that because his love for her was so strong, he would return—even if his life was taken in battle, and it was to be only in spirit. The candle's light would guide him home."

As the girls proceeded walking on the wooded path, Sandy was so fixated on every word that Mary was saying she didn't even notice they were within fifty feet of Miller's Haunted House.

Mary continued, "For the remaining two years of the Civil War, my great-grandmother lit a candle every night, from her bedroom window. But her beloved husband never returned. Finally, she received word that, indeed, he had been killed in battle, but the body was never recovered. My great-grandmother sought spiritual guidance to help bring back the spirit of her dead husband, so he could finally be at peace. But his spirit never returned. As she grew into an old lady, she continued to light the candle, never giving up her hope.

"On her deathbed, she made her oldest son promise not to sell this farm or the house, so that one day she might finally be united in spirit with her husband. Only after their reunion occurred, could the house and the property be sold."

A Monarch butterfly landed softly on Mary's book bag. She paused in her storytelling, and gently put her finger near it. The butterfly crawled onto it and remained there, as if, it too, was listening. Mary's eyes focused back on Sandy's face.

"She also explained the reunion would take place after the house was naturally taken away. But if the house was destroyed in some unnatural method, the reunion couldn't take place, and there'd be a curse on the land and those living on it."

"Wow! That's quite a story, Mary!" exclaimed Sandy. "So that's why your family hasn't given in to the developers."

"Exactly. Almost every month, my parents get a knock on the door from a developer, wanting to buy our land. They say they want to build a shopping mall, and that they'll offer my parents a good price for our land. But my parents made a firm promise that it will be passed on to one of the children out of respect to their ancestors—and their fear of the curse."

Sandy and Mary had reached the house. Standing in front of the porch, Sandy questioned Mary, "But how will your family know that great-grandmother Miller has finally been united with her husband?" Her eyes nervously studied the house, and then returned to her classmate.

Mary's eyelids almost squinted closed as she peered into Sandy's eyes. "My family will know when the time has come. We'll know!"

Gradually, Sandy found herself doubting the story, as she continued staring at the haunted house, and the spell of Mary's story lifted. "Do you really believe all this, Mary? Your great-grandmother's spirit still is inside that house? I mean . . ."

All politeness vanished from Mary's voice. "Well, yes, of course! You'll see, one day they'll be together again."

Sandy had grave reservations that she'd ever see that, but the story did fascinate her. The fact that three generations still strongly believed that the spirits of their ancestors would finally find their way back to each other in this old, run-down home seemed far-fetched and unimaginable to Sandy. But at the same time, the tale intrigued her.

They resumed their journey and finally reached Mary's home. It was a big old two-story, wooden farmhouse, looking like it could use a new coat of paint. Sandy thought it had the most inviting porch she'd ever seen, the style that wrapped around the entire front and side of the house. She quickly climbed the wooden steps to sit on the old porch swing, hanging from the porch ceiling.

"Yep, Sandy, you found my favorite place," and Mary scooted next to Sandy, as they both pumped their legs to get it going.

"Wow, Mary, what a beautiful view of the wheat fields," exclaimed Sandy, as they continued swinging back and forth. The barn was off to the side, about twenty yards from the family home. Sandy saw chickens bobbing their heads back and forth in their coop, and pigs wallowing in the mud, as the late afternoon sun drifted behind a cloud. The spring air felt refreshing on her skin and in her lungs, and Sandy sighed contentedly as she glided back and forth.

Sandy could have enjoyed this for another hour, but Mary finally touched her feet to the porch floor to stop the motion. "Come on. Let's go inside."

Sandy reluctantly got off and as she stepped into Mary's house, she was taken aback by its run-down condition. The walls were cracked, and paint was peeling from them. The overstuffed green sofa and chairs looked totally worn out, but in spite of the obvious lack of money to decorate or buy new furniture, the house was kept clean and tidy. The curtains that hung in the windows were long faded, but were pulled back wide enough to allow the sun's light in, making the room welcoming and bright.

As Sandy continued her observation, she noticed various family portraits on the wall, but one in particular fascinated her. It hung on a wall by itself, and its subject was a very handsome man with light, long flowing hair, a trimmed beard, and a white robe. It looked very old and mysterious. Sandy thought it must be a picture of one of Mary's old ancestors.

"Is that a picture of your great-grandfather, the one whose spirit you're waiting for?"

"Well, in a way. That's a picture of Jesus Christ, our Savior," replied Mary.

Sandy, being Jewish and having all Jewish friends, had never seen a picture of Jesus Christ. She remembered thinking that it was strange to have it hanging on the living room wall.

Mary invited Sandy into the kitchen, where she introduced her to her mother and three younger sisters. The sisters were sitting at the kitchen table eating cookies, with milk mustaches on their upper lips. The little girls, ages two, three, and four, were giggling in between cookie bites and abandoned their snack to run and give their big sister a hug.

Henrietta, the youngest, and with chocolate stains on her checks, bellowed, "Me made cookies. Me made cookies."

Mary, taking a kitchen towel to wipe her little sister's face replied, "I can see that."

Mrs. Miller was a tall, slender, and attractive woman, with light brown hair that she wore pulled up in a bun. Today she was wearing a sleeveless cotton dress, with a full-length apron tied around her. Her attraction lay in her oval-shaped face, high cheekbones, and natural rose-colored lips, which definitely didn't need lipstick. However, to Sandy, Mrs. Miller's most prominent feature was her eyes. Sandy thought Mrs. Miller had the saddest brown eyes she had ever seen, and she wondered from where all that sadness came.

Mrs. Miller expressed her sympathy to Sandy about the loss of Beth's mother. She said, "I'll be praying for the family, asking Jesus to give them strength," and directed the girls to the kitchen counter, where dozens of delicious-looking pastries were beautifully arranged. "While you were at school today, and with the help of your little sisters, we managed to make all these. Please, help yourself."

Sandy's sweet tooth immediately focused on the lemon and strawberry tarts, which were her favorite—although the brownies covered with multi-colored sprinkles also looked tempting.

Sandy laughed, "Gosh, it's gonna be hard for me to choose. Mrs. Miller, is it okay if I eat the lemon tart? Lemon tarts are my favorite."

"Why, of course, Sandy."

Sandy took a bite. "Gee, this is the best I've ever tasted!"

"Thank you," said Mrs. Miller, "that recipe is a family secret."

After the girls finished their snack, Mary said, "The rest of these are what I'd like you to take to the Fine's." Sandy helped Mary place all the baked goods into a box, carefully arranging them so they would not be crushed. Then handing the filled box to Sandy, Mary said, "Thank you for taking it over to Beth's family."

"You can change your mind and come with me," encouraged Sandy.

"Thank you, but I'd rather not," replied Mary.

The box of pastries in hand, Sandy said good-bye to Mary's sisters and her mother, and Mary escorted her to the front door, saying, "I'll see you at school tomorrow."

When the door closed behind her, Sandy stood alone on the wraparound porch and decided to enjoy the porch swing one more time. She carefully put the box of pastries off to the side, making sure it was not in the direct path of the swing and then hopped on. After about ten minutes of swinging and enjoying both the rustic views and the breeze now blowing through her hair, she let her mind drift back over the week. It brought a shudder to her body, leaving her cold. The unexpected death of Beth's mother was a lot for her mind to untangle. She knew today represented the last day for Shivah. She had spent every available moment this week with Beth, coming over right after school and staying late into the evening. Sandy thought, *Beth is the bravest and strongest person I've ever known. She is handling everything so well.*

As she continued to swing, Sandy thought back to Tuesday, when Beth had been longing for her mother and asked Sandy to come upstairs with her, sharing personal stories about her mother that were only for the ears of her Deep Talk sister. The one that touched Sandy the most involved Beth's first week in kindergarten:

"Sandy, when I was little, I was very shy. I hated leaving my mom and going to kindergarten. On the first day of school, my mom took me and kissed me good-bye at the classroom door, but I hung on to her skirt. The kindergarten teacher whispered to my mom, but I heard her say, 'Mrs. Fine, I've handled very shy children like this before. It's time for you to let me take charge.' My mother looked my kindergarten teacher straight in the eye and said, 'I'm not leaving my daughter like this! I'll be at her side each and every day until she's comfortable.' My mom stayed with me my entire day of kindergarten, and all during the week. Then I remember playing with the children, listening to stories and going down the slide at recess. On the last day of the first week of kindergarten, when I was walking into the classroom, I turned to my mother and said, 'Mommy, I'm gonna have so much fun today!' Then I kissed her good-bye at the door."

Flies started buzzing around Sandy and she swatted at them. Several had landed on the box of pastries. She jumped off the swing. "Get away, flies!" She tucked the box under her arm, "Well, I'd better get these to Beth's, before they spoil." Feeling rushed for time, Sandy started to take the short cut to Beth's, but hesitated. *That path leads directly past the haunted house. I definitely don't wanna go that way!* She abruptly turned around and took the long route.

When she arrived, there were many visitors sitting Shivah. Lynn Ernst was there with her mother. Mrs. Ernst had come already having cooked the Fine's dinner for the evening, and was setting the food on the kitchen table. Sandy knew it was Jewish tradition that the grieving family not be responsible for cooking their meals while sitting Shivah. Relatives and friends take on this mitzvah, or good deed. Sandy brought the box of pastries into the kitchen.

When Mrs. Ernst saw Sandy, she put down the bowls she was carrying to give her a gentle embrace and in her sing-song Jewish accent asked, "What's in the box?"

"Freshly-made baked goods from one of our classmates in school. She and her family wanted me to bring this to the Fines."

Mrs. Ernst peeked into the box and when she saw the delectable-looking pastries, exclaimed, "I must go to this family for a baking lesson. These are beautiful! Why, look at these custard-strawberry tarts! Quick, let me put these away, so only Beth's family will be able to eat these! But before I do, you deserve one, Sandy, for making such a fine delivery."

Sandy didn't want to miss this opportunity in case Mrs. Ernst changed her mind, so as she put the box on the counter, she snatched the strawberry tart.

As Sandy finished eating it, Mrs. Ernst said, "*Nu*, my Kinderla, it's good?"

Sandy smacked her lips. "It definitely could take first place at a baking contest!"

With this accolade, Mrs. Ernst smiled, and collected the box of pastries from the counter to put it in a special place. "Sandy, Lynn is in the family room, with the other children."

When Lynn spotted Sandy, she rushed to her and whispered, "It's been a bad day for Beth. Right now she's in her room, saying that she needed a break from company. Maybe you can go up and talk with her?"

"Okay," responded Sandy. But as she climbed the stairs, she felt awkward and thought, *What words can I possibly say to comfort Beth?* Beth's bedroom door was closed, and Sandy knocked on it gently. She heard a quiet, "Yes?"

"It's me, Beth, Sandy. Can I come in?"

Beth came to open the door for her friend and hugged her tightly. "Sandy, I can't wait for this Shivah stuff to be over. I just wanna be left alone and to be with my family."

"Well, your prayers will be answered soon enough, because this is the last day," said Sandy.

"Yeah, well why didn't G-d answer my prayers when I was praying for my mother to get better? Where was G-d then?" Beth cried.

Sandy was taken off guard by her friend's anger, and did not know how to answer.

"It's not fair, Sandy! I'm only twelve. How could my mother leave me? She knows I still need her!"

"But, Beth," Sandy protested, "in the twelve years that you had your mother, she really cared and loved you. Until she became very ill, from what you shared with me about your mother, she was always there for you. You could tell her anything. You had a special relationship with your mom—one I wish I could have with mine."

"But at least you still have a mother!" shouted Beth. "Please, go now, Sandy. I wanna be left alone. Tell my dad I'm not coming down for dinner or the evening prayers."

Regretfully, Sandy headed downstairs to find Mr. Fine, who was sitting on the sofa, showing friends some family photos. When Sandy whispered to him what had just occurred, he excused himself to speak with his daughter. As Sandy explained the situation to Lynn, Mrs. Ernst came into the family room.

"Girls, I've laid out dinner for the family. Why don't we get our coats and let them have some time to themselves to eat and get ready for evening prayers? Sandy, would you like to come over to our house for dinner tonight?" questioned Mrs. Ernst.

"Sure. I'll just call my mom when I get to your house."

Once Sandy had telephoned home and received permission, she and Lynn immediately went to Lynn's bedroom. Lynn could see how solemn and upset her friend looked, as Sandy scrunched her body into a chair in the corner of the carpeted room.

"Do you want to talk about it, Sandy?"

"I'm worried about Beth. I've never seen her so upset."

"Sandy, we've never lost our mothers. We really can't understand everything Beth is going through. It's going to take time," Lynn responded, showing wisdom beyond her years.

"You're right," acknowledged Sandy. "Maybe she just needs some time." She stood up and lifted one of the stuffed animals off Lynn's bed and held it tight to her chest. She started pacing the room. Lynn knew Sandy had other things on her mind.

"Is there something else you want to tell me, Sandy?"

"Lynn, I've got this incredible story to tell you about Mary Miller. You're never gonna believe it."

"My girls, I've got a delicious dinner on the table," interrupted Mrs. Ernst, who was calling them from the kitchen.

Lynn's curiosity was piqued now. "You gotta tell me!"

"Well, Mary Miller's great-grandmother's spirit . . ."

"Girls, dinner is getting cold! Whatever you're talking about can continue in the kitchen," called Mrs. Ernst.

"I'll tell you after dinner; I don't want your mom to hear," Sandy said.

The two girls came to the table to feast upon a typical Eastern European Jewish meal, which included kugel, an egg noodle baked dish sweetened with apples, raisins and cinnamon, along with baked chicken and farfel, which is a pasta made out of egg barley and tossed with fried onions. Lynn, of course, was anxious to hear Sandy's story, and in her own mind came up with half a dozen scenarios as she ate. However, none could match the reality of the tale Sandy finally told her after dinner, when they were alone in Lynn's bedroom with the door shut. And as Sandy related each detail of the story, Lynn's already big, beautiful blue eyes opened wider and wider, in both amazement and disbelief.

CHAPTER 10

Graduation

Several weeks had now passed since Beth's mother died, and the scent of warm, summer days drifted in the air. Adults could be found relaxing on their comfortable lounge chairs in their backyards, catching the sun's rays on this warm, late spring day as puffy, white clouds sailed in the skies, and children delighted in their play.

"Yahoo!" yelled Lynn.

"Wow," shouted Sandy as both girls sped down Tyler's Hill on their bicycles. Lynn's long blonde hair blew every which way; Sandy's glasses bobbed up and down on her nose as her wheels bounced over the bumpy terrain.

As the girls reached the center of Tyler's field, Sandy was the first to say, "Come on. Let's do it again!" No one had to convince Lynn; she was peddling as hard as she could across the field to get back to the hill. At its foot, the girls hopped off their bikes and used all their strength to walk them back to the top.

Once there Lynn said, "After this time, we need to ride over to Beth's to see if she wants to join us."

"Already called," replied Sandy. "Beth said she didn't feel like it. She's really changed, Lynn, since her mother's death. We used to have a lot of fun together. Now, she'll barely talk to me," said Sandy, shrugging her shoulders.

"Yeah, I know what you mean. She really does keep to herself now," answered Lynn.

"I wish I could think of something to bring her out of it," insisted Sandy.

"Just give her time. That's what my mom said—Beth needs understanding and time."

"Yeah, I guess your mom's right," Sandy said, as her eyes focused on the terrain below her and she balanced herself on her bike, preparing for the exciting rollercoaster descent.

"Talking about time, can you believe it's the last day of school next Friday? I'm so excited for summer!" Lynn said, beaming.

"Are you going to camp again this year?" inquired Sandy.

"Naw. My dad's business didn't have a good year. So, I'll be around. What about you?" Lynn, moved her bike closer to Sandy, both girls ready for the next thrill ride.

"I'm staying home too," said Sandy. "We've got to come up with something good to do for the summer, so we won't be bored!"

"First, we've got to go down this hill again. Are you ready?" asked Lynn.

"Let's do it!"

They pedaled furiously then stopped, letting the force of gravity take over. They viper-gripped their handlebars, so as not to be thrown from their bicycles. Every bone in their bodies rattled and shook as they catapulted down the steep and rough terrain. This time, however, when they reached the center of the field, instead of saying, "Let's do it again," Sandy blurted out, "I know what we can do this summer!"

"What?" Lynn asked excitedly, as she sat with one foot on the ground for balance and the other on the pedal.

"We'll start a club. We'll have a special meeting place and plan secret trips, and not let our parents know!"

"Count me in! We can ask some other girls in our classroom to join, and Lisa and Elaine, who live on my block," suggested Lynn.

"The club will be a great way to get Beth up and going again!"

"You really think Beth will join?" said Lynn, squinting her eyes from the sun's glare.

"She'll probably refuse at first, but I'll keep working on her. I'm sure I can get her to join," said Sandy.

Over the next several days at school, Sandy and Lynn busily recruited girls to join their group. When Sandy approached Mary Miller, Mary said, "I'll have to ask my mom, but if she says yes, I think it'll be fun." Lynn asked several of the girls who lived on her block and before long the count was up to seven, with the hope that more would soon join. Sandy finally approached Beth during art class, trying her best pitch, "Beth, I have something really exciting to tell you!"

Beth was working on her drawing and seemed totally uninterested in what Sandy had to say. She reluctantly stopped drawing and looked up. Finally, halfheartedly, she asked, "What is it?"

"Lynn and I have started a summer club. We're going to go on secret travels, have cookouts, and go on camping trips. Already, seven girls have joined!"

"I'm really not interested," replied Beth, turning away from Sandy.

"Ah, come on, Beth! We're gonna have a lot of fun!"

"I'd rather just stay close to home and work on my art." Beth returned her focus to her drawing, avoiding eye contact with Sandy.

Sandy could hear the sadness in Beth's voice, see it in her body language. Sandy's feelings were not hurt when Beth rejected joining the club. She had anticipated this, and she knew somehow she'd figure out a way to pull Beth out of her depression and into the group.

However, today when Sandy returned from school, she had to put her plans for the summer on hold and be concerned about tomorrow—the last day of school. As Student Council President, she was given the responsibility of preparing a speech for her Sixth Grade Graduation Ceremony. Sandy had been working on it for the last couple of evenings at the desk in her bedroom. She wrote the speech five different ways, and each time she read it out loud, she thought, *Gee, this sounds really corny!* She'd immediately crunch it into a ball and throw it into the trash. The trash can was now filled to the top. Her anxiety was rising and she was feeling again that the most recent draft did not convey what she wanted to say. It, too, got balled up and thrown into the trash. She was growing tired and frustrated, as it was already past midnight. She was just about to rewrite it for the sixth time when she heard Linda come in the front door with her date.

Sandy thought to herself, *Fantastic—now that Linda's home, she'll be able to help me with this darn speech!* She waited a few minutes, but when Linda didn't come into the bedroom, Sandy growing impatient, peeked out the bedroom door—to see Linda kissing Daniel good night, in the front hallway. Sandy shrugged in disgust; she was hoping Linda would be cooling it by now with Daniel, the photographer, and get more interested in Robert, the pre-med student, whom Sandy liked much better.

Sandy thought, *This good-bye thing has lasted long enough!* So, to expedite the matter, she strolled into the kitchen, pretending she was hungry. This obviously had the reaction she wanted, because as soon as she entered the living room to cut through to the kitchen, Linda and Daniel stopped kissing. Linda, thinking everyone in the house was asleep, was startled by seeing her sister, and hissed, "I thought you were sleeping!"

Sandy, grinning, replied, "Oh no, I've been working on my graduation speech all evening, and now I'm starving! Daniel, would you like something to eat?"

Daniel thought Linda's sister was a brat, and if he could tell it to Sandy's face and still keep Linda as a girlfriend he would, but he knew better. He revealed his irritation about the situation when he brusquely put on his jacket and hurried out the door saying to Linda, "I'll just call you tomorrow." Linda said good night, and furiously went into the bedroom, where Sandy showed up one minute later, with milk and cookies.

"Would you like some?" inquired Sandy.

Linda growled, "No! And I can't believe you came out into the living room! Why aren't you asleep, like all the other sixth grade girls in the neighborhood?"

"They're snug as a bug in their beds because they don't have to worry about a graduation speech tomorrow, the way I have to!" cried Sandy. "What I've written is terrible. I just can't get it to sound right!"

"Your graduation from elementary school is tomorrow?"

"Yes!" snapped Sandy.

Linda, suddenly feeling sympathetic for Sandy's situation said, "Here, let me take a look at what you've written."

Sandy frantically looked through the trash and pulled out the most recent draft. She unfolded the scrunched up ball, like a child slowly unwrapping the last piece of stale Halloween candy: the child really doesn't want it, but eats the piece anyway, because that's all that's left. And some candy is better than no candy. Sandy, ambivalent, handed the speech over to Linda.

Linda sat on her bed with a book on her lap, pressing the speech flat with her hands, working on getting the creases out, so she could read it. She moved the lamp closer to the bed, casting a yellow glow over the speech. After a few minutes she looked up at Sandy. "You're right. This does need work!"

Confirming what Sandy already knew did not help matters, and it brought her to tears. "See, I told you! I told you it was terrible! Now, I'm gonna make a fool out of myself!"

Linda, being the loving big sister that she was, assured her saying, "Not if I can help it!"

Over the next few hours, the two sisters worked together, fixing Sandy's address. It was now 2:00 a.m. Linda was putting on the finishing touches and proudly announced, "Okay, Sandy. Now, I think it's ready."

Sandy, sleepy and red eyed, got up from her bed and read the speech, pretending to be delivering it at the Graduation Assembly. When she finished, Linda, sitting on the edge of her bed, applauded. "That sounds really good, sis!"

"That's because you wrote it!" beamed Sandy.

"No, it was a joint effort! I loved your last line" . . . and in an overly-affected manner—"Mr. Avery, teachers, and parents, you have given us a foundation on which to build our future academic and social successes. For that, I and my fellow classmates are indeed grateful."

Sandy had to admit she liked it, too.

"Thanks, Linda, for helping me out. Are you coming tomorrow?"

"Sure! Now that I know about it!" Linda replied.

"Well, lately, you're always out on a date!" complained Sandy.

"Tomorrow, I'll play hooky from my college classes and come to see you deliver your speech!"

"You mean our speech," said Sandy, now embracing her sister.

Linda held up the half-filled cup of milk that was still on the nightstand, and gestured as if she was making a great toast, "To our speech!" she exclaimed. And with that, the two sisters finally got into bed and called it a night.

"Linda," said Sandy quietly, lying comfortably underneath the blanket on her twin bed.

"Yes?"

"One thing I know I'm not gonna be when I grow up," whispered Sandy.

"What's that?" asked Linda.

"A writer."

"You know that old adage, never say never!" said Linda wisely.

"What are you saying? Without your help, I never could've pulled off writing this speech!" insisted Sandy.

"Even the best writers need an editor," said Linda.

"Really?"

"Really. Just consider me your editor, and besides, that's why big sisters are so much fun to have around. And I know you'll help me out with Mom or Dad, when I'm coming home late from a date. You can tell them I'm at Sherry's house."

"Absolutely! Will you be needing to go to Sherry's house to 'study' until 2:00 a.m. this weekend?" asked Sandy.

"No. Not this weekend, but maybe next." Linda, now, too, lying in her bed, puffed up her pillow and settled her head comfortably into it.

" 'Roger' that," said Sandy, "or should I say, 'Daniel' that?"

"Sandy, for now, just say GOOD NIGHT!"

"Good night, Linda. I love you."

"I love you, too, my little sister."

Sandy rose early graduation morning. She'd barely had five hours of sleep, but she didn't feel tired. She was excited about graduation and wanted to review her speech in the living room one more time, before her family awakened. Feeling comfortable with her address, she returned to the bedroom to choose an outfit. The room was still dark and Linda was sleeping soundly. Sandy didn't want to turn on the bedroom light, disturbing her sister's rest, so she quietly pulled up the window shade. The morning's gentle white glow rushed into the room and Sandy now had enough light to see inside the closet she shared with her sister. She picked a dress that still had a sales tag hanging from a sleeve. She cut it off and put on the dress. Then she walked over to the full-length mirror attached to the back of the bedroom door. Upon seeing her reflection, she thought this, indeed, was a good choice.

Mr. Lowenthal came into the room to wake up his younger daughter and was surprised to see Sandy up. "I see you're already dressed."

"Oh, Dad, I'm too excited to sleep. You like this dress?" inquired Sandy, as she twirled around modeling it for him.

"You look like a beauty queen, dear," said Mr. Lowenthal, and gave his daughter a kiss on the forehead.

All the talking woke Linda. She rubbed her eyes and shrieked, "That's my new dress! You can't wear that, Sandy! Take it off, now! Dad, tell her she can't wear my dress!"

"But, Dad," pleaded Sandy, "Mom didn't take me shopping. And I don't have anything nice to wear! Can't I just borrow it for my graduation, just this once?"

"NO!" screamed Linda. "Take it off, now!"

"Oh, come on," begged Sandy, "Linda, please?"

"No! I'm wearing it next weekend for Daniel's photography show," insisted Linda.

Sandy now turned to her dad for support. "Dad, please tell her something!"

"Okay, girls, that's enough fighting," demanded Mr. Lowenthal. Then he turned to Linda. "Now, how old are you? And how old is your baby sister?"

"Dad, that's what you always say!" yelled Linda, as she darted like a cannonball to the closet frantically looking through. "Here, Sandy, what about this one? It's beautiful!"

"That dress doesn't fit me anymore," cried Sandy, with tears running down her cheeks.

Linda, suddenly realizing that she was going to lose this battle, finally gave in. Reluctantly, she gave out a loud sigh and said, "All right, but just this once. You can borrow this dress just because it's your graduation. Understand, Sandy?"

"I promise, just this once!" replied Sandy gratefully, running to the bathroom to brush her hair for the tenth time that morning.

While Sandy was in the bathroom, Mr. Lowenthal, standing in the bedroom doorway, complimented his older daughter. "Linda, I'm very proud of you, for being so mature and understanding."

With less enthusiasm, Linda responded, "Thanks, Dad. After all, I know it's a big day for her."

"That's why we call you the professor of the house. You understand when something is more important than a material object. Now, it's more important that we help Sandy feel good about her graduation day," Mr. Lowenthal said.

"Okay. I understand Dad," said Linda, and she turned away from her father to pick out something to wear herself.

"You're coming this morning?" questioned Mr. Lowenthal.

"Yeah. I just have to get dressed and eat a quick breakfast," replied Linda, who was now looking for a pair of shoes to match.

Her graduation was one of Sandy's most exhilarating experiences. She felt and looked beautiful, and was so very proud of how she delivered her graduation speech. The fact that Sandy's mother couldn't attend because she was at a Bible Assembly in another city did not upset her, since she knew her dad, sister, and brother were present. In fact, Sandy was certain that after presenting her speech, although she could not see her family members in the audience, she could distinctly hear the clapping coming directly from them to her.

Sandy could barely contain her excitement when Mr. Avery, the principal, called her name. She strode to the stage and proudly received her graduation certificate. But when she sat back down, she suddenly realized that this truly meant good-bye. Good-bye to the only school she had known since kindergarten. Good-bye to the school where she had become Student Council President, where she had made wonderful friends, and had great teachers. A tear edged its way from the corner of her eye and down her check. Sandy suddenly realized good-byes hurt.

CHAPTER 11

The Club

It had not even been a week since Sandy had graduated from elementary school and she and Lynn were already busy organizing their summer club. The two were on the phone discussing details about it.

"Yeah, this Friday for our club's first meeting sounds great! By the way, is Mary Miller joining?" Lynn asked.

"I'll find out today and let you know," replied Sandy, sitting at the kitchen table, with sunbeams pouring through the window.

"We still don't have a name, yet," said Lynn, sitting cross-legged on her family room floor, the phone up to her right ear.

"Maybe that's something we can come up with at the first meeting," answered Sandy, one hand holding the phone to her ear and the other flipping through magazines, looking for an idea to name the club.

"Sure. We'll figure out something then," said Lynn. "I'll see you on Friday at 9:00 a.m., at my garage."

"You betcha!" said Sandy.

When Sandy hung up, she pushed the magazines aside and ran out the door to ride her bicycle to Mary Miller's house. Instead of going the long way, she decided to take the shortcut, through the woods—past Miller's Haunted House. As she sighted the dilapidated homestead, she felt very different about it, now knowing its "secret." Somehow, she felt connected to it. She couldn't explain this strange new feeling, but she felt as if the house was calling to her.

As she drew nearer, she got off her bicycle and climbed the rickety stairs to the front porch. With each step she took, the old wooden planks made that familiar creaking sound. As she peered through a dirty window, Sandy found it as she'd seen it the first time. Nothing appeared different, except that the old, worn-out Bible sitting on the table was now opened. She thought she remembered last time, when she'd looked through the window, seeing the book's worn cover. Yes. She was sure it had been closed. She saw no sign of movement and was just about to leave when suddenly she thought she saw someone move inside. Her heart skipped ten beats; her face went chalk white with fright. She ran from the house quicker than a jackrabbit fleeing from a fox, jumped back onto her bike, and pedaled furiously to Mary's house.

She arrived panting, and with her knees still shaking. She pounded on the door. When Mary answered and saw how distressed her friend looked, she quickly brought her inside. "I'll get you some water." Mary took Sandy's trembling hand, escorting her to a chair at the kitchen table.

"What's wrong, Sandy? You look like you've just seen a ghost."

"How did you know?" Sandy exclaimed, obviously still shaken by what she had just seen.

"Tell me about it," Mary said, with heightened anticipation in her voice.

Sandy told Mary about the experience, as Mary sat listening attentively. When Sandy finished, Mary said, "Now it's just you and my dad who've seen my great-grandmother's ghost."

"Your dad's seen her?" questioned Sandy.

"I've gone at least a thousand times. And I've never seen her once! You should feel proud that she showed herself to you," answered Mary, with a slight spark of envy in her voice.

"Proud? How about scared to death!" exclaimed Sandy. "I don't believe all this ghost hocus-pocus stuff for a minute! I'm sure there's some perfectly sensible explanation for what I saw," declared Sandy.

"Well, then, believe what you want," replied Mary, holding her chin high.

Now that her nerves were more settled, Sandy was able to focus on what she originally intended to ask. "Our first club meeting will be this Friday. Are you joining, Mary?"

"My mother first said no," replied Mary, "because I must help out on the farm, and take care of my little brother in the afternoons. But when I told my dad about it, he was able to convince my mom that I still would have plenty of time to do my chores, and on the days that the club meets, my younger sister can help take care of my brother. She knows how to give him his medicines, too."

"Great!" exclaimed Sandy. "I'm so glad your dad was able to convince your mom. But what's wrong with your brother?"

Stammering, Mary explained, "He's got . . . childhood... childhood leukemia." Shaking her head, she continued, "Doctors say there's nothing more they can do for him. Except my dad learned there's one place using special high-risk treatments, but we can't afford them."

The girls' conversation was interrupted by a loud knocking at the door and Mary's mom calling out from upstairs, "Mary, can you get that?"

Mary excused herself from the kitchen table to answer the door. Opening it, she said, "Wait," to the two men standing there and called upstairs, "Mom, they want to talk with you."

The two men—in gray suits with briefcases held to their sides—were not invited in. However, they waited patiently on the wooden wraparound porch, standing behind the screened front door until Mrs. Miller came to speak with them. Mary returned to the kitchen where Sandy, still sitting at the kitchen table, overheard Mrs. Miller's conversation.

"Look, I thought my husband told you we're not interested in selling the farm! Please stop coming over and bothering us!" Then Sandy heard Mrs. Miller slam the door closed, and run upstairs crying.

There was an awkward silence between the two girls, and Sandy knew she was pushing proper etiquette when she said, "But, if you sell the farm to the developers, you'd have the money to help your brother—and probably plenty of money left over. Your family would be rich!" insisted Sandy.

"And risk the rest of the family being cursed, because my great-grandmother's house would be unnaturally destroyed by the developers! They would come with their bulldozers and in less than an hour tear it down."

"You really can't believe in this curse thing?" said Sandy, getting up from the kitchen table and walking over to look out the bay windows near the front door.

"Of course we do," Mary said, following Sandy into the living room. "I know it's hard for you to understand, but as a family that's how we feel!" exclaimed Mary.

Sandy felt she had overstepped her boundaries in giving her opinion about selling the farm, and sensed it was time to leave. "So, I'll see you this Friday at Lynn's, for our first club meeting?"

Shaking her head no, Mary replied, "I can't make the first one, but the following week I can."

With that information, Sandy opened the front door, said good-bye to her friend and left, hopping back on her bike. This time Sandy was taking the long way home—making sure to avoid the house in the woods. As she rode home, she thought, *I'll stop at Beth's house and try one last time to get her to join.*

When she arrived, Beth's sister told her Beth was upstairs. Sandy found the bedroom door open and entered, finding her friend working quietly at her desk. Not noticing Sandy, Beth continued drawing. Sandy feigned a cough intending to break Beth's concentration, and Beth, looking up expecting to see her sister, smiled, happily, surprised to see her friend sitting on the edge of her bed. "Sandy, I'm so glad you've come over!"

"What are you drawing, Beth?" inquired Sandy.

"I'm almost finished with the sketch, come see," said Beth. "I'm really proud of it."

Sandy got up from Beth's bed, walked over to the desk and peered over Beth's shoulder. Beth was drawing a picture of herself and her mother. Her mother was poised beautifully on an elegant chair, with Beth sitting on one of its arms, leaning lovingly into her mother, with one hand resting on her mother's shoulder.

"Mom promised just the two of us would take a professional picture, when she was feeling well again, but, well, you know—" sadly said Beth. "When I'm finished, it'll be my first oil on canvas work."

Sandy knew Beth at twelve was already a talented artist, but now she was even more convinced that one day her friend's talents would be known far and wide. Sandy was moved by the drawing and also by the renewed realization of how much Beth missed her mother.

"This is an exquisite drawing!" exclaimed Sandy.

"I'm going to give it to my father, for his birthday in three months," responded Beth, as she continued working on the drawing.

"He'll cherish it forever," answered Sandy.

Sandy felt it was now time to bring up again the subject of Beth joining the club. But she wondered how she would convince her friend, when Beth was still in so much grief. Sandy thought of enticing her by telling her about Miller's Haunted House, and the strange incident that had happened earlier today—how the club might investigate what was truly behind this peculiar occurrence. But she felt the timing was wrong. Instead, she relayed the story of Mary Miller's brother, and planted the seeds for thinking about how the club might be able to help the family in some way. Sandy suggested coming up with some great fundraising idea, so Mary's brother would be able to obtain the special medical treatments. But the more Sandy talked, the more disinterested Beth appeared, until finally Sandy was getting so frustrated she yelled, "Beth, you haven't said a word about the situation! Have you heard what I said?"

Beth put her art supplies down, got up from the desk, faced her friend, and yelled back, "I've heard you! And I don't wanna' join. It's stupid!"

"The club or helping Mary's brother?" questioned Sandy.

"Both! They're stupid ideas!"

"No they're not!" insisted Sandy, who now pushed herself within two inches of Beth's nose, her own nostrils flaring.

"Mary's brother can't be helped—he's a goner! Just like my mother—doctors can't help him!" raged Beth, with her eyes now looking like they were on fire.

"But maybe they can!" Sandy insisted.

"Well, if that's how you want to spend your time this summer—just go. Leave!" cried Beth. "I won't be a part of it!"

"But, Beth! I've started this club because of you. I thought you'd finally join us. Now, we can all try and help Mary's . . ."

"Well, you guessed wrong," replied Beth, and turned her back on Sandy.

Angrily, Sandy erupted, "I guess I did!" She bounded down the steps two at a time, leaving Beth alone in her bedroom and quickly hopped on her bicycle. A trail of anger followed her as she headed home. She parked her bike on the side of her house and stormed inside.

Once there, she quickly called Lynn from her bedroom phone. "Lynn, I just got home from Beth's. No deal with her joining the club. Talking with her was like walking on a land mine! She's become impossible. I can't get her to budge!"

"The summer is just beginning, perhaps she'll come around," Lynn said.

"Maybe, but I doubt it. Beth can be very stubborn."

"Remember, Beth lost her mother—we haven't lost ours."

The girls said good-bye and got off the phone. Sandy thought about what Lynn had said and wanted to call Beth to tell her she was sorry that they had the fight, but pride got in the way.

CHAPTER 12

The Curse

At 6:15 a.m., Mary Miller's sandaled feet were wet with dew by the time she arrived at the old wooden barn to do her chores. She entered the barn, and its sweet smells of hay dust and cattle feed mixed with the strong scent of manure wafted through the air and up through her nostrils, helping her shake off her sleepiness on this bright, breezy summer day. The spiders' webs crisscrossed in the rafters glistened, when a ray of sunshine sneaked through the cracks of the old barn's facades. Mary's two older brothers were already in the barn's loft, pitching hay down the shaft, where Mary collected and distributed it to the cows and sheep—restlessly shifting in their stalls, mooing and baaing for their morning feeding.

"Mary, you're thirty minutes late," Mr. Miller said sternly.

"I'm sorry, Dad. It was really hard getting out of bed this morning. I was helping Mom with Timothy late into the evening and—"

"That should be your biggest problem in life!" snapped Mr. Miller. "This will be the last morning you come to the barn late! Understand, young lady?"

"Yes, Father. It won't happen again. I promise," replied Mary, as she held several flakes of hay in her arms.

"No more time for talking. There's work to be done," chided her father.

Mary had occasionally been late coming to the barn in the past and her father never berated her. She was surprised by his sudden irritability. All week, he barked out commands at the children. Mary wondered what was really provoking her father's new temper. Mary had to hurry along feeding and watering the livestock, in order to avoid evoking the ire of her father. She disliked these changes in him, longing for his old ways—when he was gentle and understanding.

During the summer months, when school was out, all the Miller children were expected to do several chores in helping to maintain the farm. Mr. Miller couldn't afford to pay a farmhand's wages. The children may not have liked it, but they didn't complain. They loved their family farm just as much as their parents did. After Mary helped feed the animals, she collected two dozen freshly laid eggs from the chicken coop, for their morning's breakfast. To avoid breakage, she gently placed them in the basket her mother had given her, and before she headed home, she delivered a message to her father.

"Mom says breakfast will be late this morning, at 7:15."

"She knows I hate eating breakfast late!" He clamped his jaws tight and the veins on his neck bulged, as he put gasoline into his tractor, readying it to cultivate the cornfields. Mr. Miller often worked twelve hours a day, even more in the summer months, and especially long hours during harvest time. When Sandy first met Mr. Miller, she thought he could never be a contestant on the popular game show, "What's My Line," because his weather-beaten face, rough hands, and Herculean physique would instantly give him away as a hardworking Midwestern farmer.

Mary entered the kitchen hearing sounds of coffee percolating and the sweet aroma of freshly baked biscuits wafting through the air, as her mother took them from the oven. Mary brought the fresh eggs to the kitchen countertop and immediately started helping her mother prepare the meal. When the Miller family sat down to eat their big hearty breakfast of scrambled eggs, bacon, and the warm biscuits, there was an empty chair at the head of the table. Mr. Miller never missed a breakfast before, not until this morning. He was always the first to say, "A farmer and his family need a proper meal, to be able to attend to all the work that needs to be done on a farm. Yes, the breakfast is, indeed, the most important meal of the day!"

"Mary, you told your father breakfast would be late today?" asked Mary's mother.

"Yes, Ma'am, I told him," replied Mary, lowering her head.

Mary clearly saw that her father's absence at the breakfast table upset her mother, when she put a huge helping on his plate and every few minutes went to the kitchen window, to see if her husband was coming. Mrs. Miller's tenseness and apparent anxiety caused the children to eat their breakfast in silence, as opposed to the typical chatter and clatter always heard around the table.

All this week after the Miller children were in bed, Mary had heard her father speak in hushed, quick tones to his wife, and then quietly leave the house. Mary thought she heard her mother crying after these nightly conversations, but she wasn't sure. She stayed up waiting for her father's return, which was usually within an hour. When he did return, he always lit the fireplace. Each evening, Mary sneaked downstairs to see her father pacing the floor. She knew her father was terribly worried about something—and that something made her mother cry nightly. Mary was determined to find out what her parents were hiding.

The next evening, she secretively followed her father. Sure enough, he headed to where she had anticipated—his grandmother's house. Mr. Miller turned on a flashlight, inadvertently allowing Mary, through the window, to witness her father pacing up and down in the old house. She saw his brows were furrowed and his lips moved, as if he was apparently speaking to someone. Mary desperately wanted to hear, but she'd have to climb up the old, rickety, wooden steps to get closer, revealing her presence. And that would result in a definite punishment for being out of bed.

As Mary reviewed her options, she noticed a side window ajar. She approached it and crouched down. Light from a crescent moon revealed her caved in face, as Mary listened to her father's strained voice. The words caused Mary's body to tremble.

"Grandmother Miller, I've come all week to talk to your spirit, and you've ignored me. Perhaps it's because you feel my heavy heart—already know what I must say. For weeks, I've agonized over this decision. Martha and I have cried for several nights about it." Then, Mr. Miller paused for a long time. Mary heard her father pace once more, as the floorboards creaked under his weight. Finally, the shocking words poured out of him like a sudden bursting rain cloud. "We must sell the Miller farm."

Mary's heart locked up and she felt as though the blood stopped coursing through her veins—like a heart patient suddenly pulled off the ventilator before last rites were spoken. This revelation shook her to the core. She felt hopelessly betrayed. She thought, *No matter how bad things are for my family, my parents promised never to sell the farm! Never!* She was horrified at the news, and then she heard more of what her father said.

"Please, Grandmother Miller, understand it's not for selfish motives, but we need money to save Timothy's life. We must pay doctors in order for Timothy to receive specialized treatments for his illness. Please understand—"

Mary threw her hands over her ears. She had heard enough. Guided by the light of the stars, she dashed back to the house and slipped inside, tip-toeing up to her bedroom, which she shared with three younger sisters. They were all sound asleep. Mary quickly got in bed. Her heart was beating like a trapped animal. She lay awake all night, now knowing what her parents had been hiding from her and the rest of her siblings.

Waves of shame washed over her. She desperately wanted her brother to get help, but struggled with the implications. She was petrified of the unknown consequences of her great-grandmother's curse for selling the property, before the spirits were at peace. She felt hopeless. She had to confide in someone, but whom? She thought, *Even if I did tell, how could anyone convince my father that he mustn't sell the farm for money—no matter what? My father is very stubborn. Once his mind is made up—look out!*

Since it was a sleepless night for her, Mary arrived at the barn early to do her chores, trying to avoid her father. She didn't want to face him now, knowing his intentions. She hurriedly gathered the two dozen eggs from the chicken coop, and brought it to the kitchen to assist with breakfast. Mary was beating eggs, when she heard the doorbell ring. She ran to open the door to the same men, who only a couple of weeks earlier her mother had asked to leave—the developers.

The two men, dressed in gray suits, politely asked to speak to her mother. Mary called her, and Mrs. Miller quickly came to the front door, wiping her hands on her apron. Seeing who it was, she chose to talk with them on the porch, pulling the door shut behind her, so the children wouldn't hear. But Mary knew. *They're here—to demolish great-grandmother Miller's house, invoking the curse on all of my family!*

CHAPTER 13

Dr. Stone

On the morning of the first meeting of the club, the sky's dark clouds released a deluge of rain. "Oh great," Sandy said aloud, looking out of her bedroom window, "this isn't a good day for the meeting!" Nevertheless, when she arrived at Lynn's garage, umbrella in hand, seven girls were present—eager to be club members. Sandy was troubled about Beth's absence, but relieved that Mary was absent today, because Sandy didn't know Mary's feelings regarding the club trying to help her family. Before that happened, however, Sandy needed everyone's approval, or at least a majority. Sandy called the meeting to order. She felt comfortable being the chairperson of a meeting, since she had performed these duties during the school year as Student Council president. And with the extra tips she'd received from Mr. Avery, the principal, she knew how to handle a variety of issues arising from meetings. Sandy passed out the agenda that she had pulled together last night, and it was unanimously approved. The first item was to choose a name for the club. After discussing a variety of possibilities, the final vote revealed that the name "Club Sisters" had won out.

The next item on the agenda was an explanation by Sandy to her club sisters about Mary's brother's illness, and the idea that if they raised the funds, they'd be in a position to assist the family in obtaining medical care.

Elaine said, "It's a great idea, but it's a lot of money to raise—just over the summer!"

The girls continued discussing the issue in their "Club House." Though it was now pouring rain, it was one of those "straight down" rains, so the girls didn't have to close the garage doors against any wind, and were able to remain nice and dry.

Sandy thought it was actually pleasant to have a meeting like this in Lynn's garage, while it was raining so heavily. Had it not been for today's meeting, she was certain they'd be bored out of their minds, cooped up at home. Suddenly, Lynn stood up and yelled, "Beth—come on in!"

Everyone stopped talking; they were surprised to see Beth, holding an umbrella over her head, standing outside the garage. Sandy was so happy to see Beth that she ran and gave her a great big hug and exclaimed, "Beth, you made it! I knew you'd come."

"I'm joining the club on one condition," insisted Beth.

"What's that?" questioned Sandy.

"We help Mary's brother my way," demanded Beth.

"And what way is that?" asked Lynn.

Beth, folding down her umbrella and entering the garage said to the girls, "Forget the fundraising idea—there's no time! If we're going to help Mary's brother it has to be now! He needs medical treatment soon! It could already be too late!"

"But we don't know any doctor that'll take him without medical insurance!" exclaimed Lynn.

"Beth, Mary told me that their family is seeking specialized treatments that many doctors aren't using," said Sandy.

"I'll call my mother's doctor; she'll know how to help," assured Beth.

"Then let's call now!" urged Sandy. "Lynn, can we go inside your house and make a call?"

"Sure, my mother won't mind."

All the girls, huddling and giggling under three umbrellas, dashed through the rain toward Lynn's back door. Mrs. Ernst was delighted to see them all file in after stamping their feet dry on the hall mat. She welcomed them in that familiar sing-song Jewish accent, "Oh, girls, it's good to see you. I'm glad you've come inside. How about some milk and cookies?"

"Mom," Lynn said, "we just came in for a minute, because we need to use the phone."

"Sure, my Lynny, dear. Use the phone in the den," suggested Mrs. Ernst. "You'll have the most privacy."

All the girls crammed into the small den. Some sat on the couch; some on the floor. They were all feeling good about being involved in a plan that could help Mary's brother. Beth dialed information to get the telephone number of Dr. Catherine Stone. Then she dialed the doctor's office. Hearing a receptionist's voice answer, she said, "Hello, this is Beth Fine. I need to speak with Dr. Stone."

"Dr. Stone is seeing a patient. She can return the call—"

"No, I'll wait!" insisted Beth. "But please, tell her this is Sara Fine's daughter. I must speak to her right away!"

"All right, I'll tell her. Please hold," answered the receptionist.

Impatiently, Sandy asked, "Will the doctor talk to you?"

"I'm on hold," answered Beth, as she began twisting her curls around her fingers.

Five minutes later, Dr. Stone came on the line. "Beth Fine?"

"Yes, Dr. Stone, it's me," answered Beth, as she continued to twirl her curls with her index finger, sitting on the edge of the couch.

"It's good to hear from you. How have you been?" inquired Dr. Stone.

"Dr. Stone, I'm calling about an important matter. There's a little boy who is sick—like my mother was, and he needs your help."

"But doesn't he have a doctor that is already treating him?"

"Not really. Not anymore. I mean . . .you see the family . . . well, it's the insurance."

"What kind of insurance, Beth, does the family have?" questioned Dr. Stone.

"Well, they don't."

"They have no medical insurance of any kind?" She put down her medical book on the desk.

"That's right," said Beth, biting her lower lip.

"I see," said Dr. Stone, and she pushed her head back against the chair and sighed into the phone.

"Won't you help?" pleaded Beth, holding her breath.

"How about coming to see me next week? And we can discuss more about this case," said Dr. Stone.

"Well . . . what about . . .tomorrow?" questioned Beth.

"Sorry, Beth. The soonest I can speak to you about this is next Thursday—"

"Please, Dr. Stone, I need to speak to you soon!"

"Beth, my schedule is full for tomorrow. I could see—"

"Dr. Stone, I promise I won't take much of your time. Please!" pleaded Beth.

"Give me a minute, Beth." Dr. Stone put the phone to the side and looked at her next day's schedule. Her appointment book indicated that she had a forty-five-minute consultation with a patient scheduled for 10:00 a.m., and another patient scheduled for 11:00 a.m. She picked up the receiver. "All right, Beth. Come tomorrow morning at 10:45. It'll have to be brief, Beth. And please, don't be late."

"I won't. Thank you, Dr. Stone!" Beth put down the phone. All the girls asked simultaneously, "What did the doctor say?"

"She'll talk with me tomorrow," relayed Beth, her face and eyes revealing her emotional strain.

"Great! Beth, I'm sure you'll be able to convince her to help!" said Sandy excitedly.

"I hope so," replied Beth. "But who will drive me?"

"I'll ask my sister," said Sandy. "I'm sure she'll do us this favor."

The girls thought it inappropriate for every club member to go to see Dr. Stone tomorrow, so they appointed Sandy to be Beth's partner.

Sandy's sister Linda readily agreed to drive the girls to Dr. Stone's office the next day. She dropped them off promptly at 10:30 a.m., saying she'd return in an hour. The two girls entered the crowded elevator, and Beth pressed the tenth-floor button. Exiting the elevator, Sandy followed Beth to an office at the end of the well-lit corridor. The girls entered, seeing several people sitting in the waiting area. Beth nervously approached the receptionist, telling her her name and that she was here to see Dr. Stone. The receptionist asked Beth to take a seat. Sandy and Beth both sat down. Beth started twisting her curls again. Sandy reached for a magazine lying on the table and started flipping the pages. Beth was becoming impatient. She sat for five minutes and than sprang up from her chair, pacing back and forth inside the waiting room.

Sandy sensed being back in Dr. Stone's office was bringing back painful memories for her friend. Walking over to Beth, Sandy whispered in her ear, "I know this must be hard for you," squeezing her hand. Beth appreciated her friend's understanding. Just then, the nurse called out Beth's name and showed both girls into Dr. Stone's office, where she sat working. Upon seeing Beth, she put down her pen and came around her desk to give her a warm embrace. "You know, we did everything we could to try and save your mom."

"I know," Beth said, holding back the tears. "This is my friend, Sandy Lowenthal."

"Nice to meet you, Sandy," replied Dr. Stone. "Girls, please sit down." And she escorted them to two comfortable leather chairs, across from her desk. After they both were seated, Dr. Stone noticed that Beth was agitated and gently said to her, "Now, let's talk about this special family you know."

Beth relayed the story of Mary Miller's brother, and how the family was poor and did not have health coverage for the special medical treatments that the little boy needed. Sandy added to the discussion by telling Dr. Stone what a proud family the Millers were and how they'd never ask for charity. Dr. Stone listened intently, sitting across from the girls and leaning forward with interest.

When they had finished their story Dr. Stone said, "Girls, I'm very touched you want to help this family."

The doctor slowly stood up and walked over to the window. Her back now facing the girls, she glanced out the window, watching the people leaving and entering the medical building. As Beth sat twisting her curls, staring at Dr. Stone's back, Sandy noticed the gentle morning sunlight pushing a beam of light through the wooden blinds and falling onto the carpeted floor in front of Dr. Stone's desk. Dr. Stone turned and faced the girls.

"I'm willing to take the case, if the parents will come in with the child to see me. And they won't have to worry about financial concerns."

Beth was so excited she jumped up from her seat. "Thank you, Dr. Stone. When can you see them?"

"This Friday," she replied. "The sooner I see the child the better."

Beth ran over to the doctor and embraced her. "I knew you'd help us!"

"Girls, you must understand, I make no promises. There is no guarantee in this business."

"We understand," said Beth, wiping a tear from her eye.

Sandy's sister arrived and the girls climbed into the back seat; they were grinning from ear to ear. Linda pulled out of the parking lot in her red Nash Rambler, and out onto the busy street. Five minutes later, at the red light, Linda looked in her rearview mirror and noticed the girls were quiet, but still had that huge grin on their faces. Linda couldn't bear the suspense any longer.

"Well, Sandy, are you going to tell me why you and Beth have this huge smile plastered on your faces?"

"Well, only if you can keep a secret," replied Sandy.

"Sandy, I should be offended by that comment," said Linda. "Of course I can!"

"Promise not to tell Mom or Dad?"

"I promise," she said, as she continued to drive down the street.

"And for sure you can't tell Frank."

"For sure. I promise," said Linda.

"And definitely, I mean definitely, not your lover boy, Daniel, the photographer!"

"Okay, okay, Sandy, I promise! Now are you going to tell me why I had to drive you and Beth to the Northland Medical Center in such a hurry?"

Sandy and Beth took turns explaining to Linda why it was critical to talk with Dr. Stone this morning and not miss their appointment. Linda nodded her head approvingly. "I just pray it'll all work out. You girls are doing a great thing."

When the girls returned to Sandy's home, Mary Miller, with a grave look on her face, was pedaling up the side driveway on her bicycle, out of breath from riding her bike so fast. Sandy noticed that Mary's face looked distraught and her eyes had a misty, glazed look to them. "Mary, what's wrong?"

Looking at Sandy, she said anxiously, "I must speak with you alone, Sandy."

"Hey, we're all 'Club Sisters'. We can't keep secrets from each other," Sandy replied.

"All right," Mary said reluctantly, as she dismounted from her bike and joined the girls to enter Sandy's house.

The three girls went immediately into Sandy's bedroom and sat on the floor in a little triangle at the base of the bed. It wasn't until Sandy jumped up to close the door that Mary felt comfortable enough to tell them the terrible news, "We're all going to be cursed!"

"What are you talking about?" questioned Beth.

"My father has agreed to sell the farm to the developers!" cried Mary.

"But he can't!" exclaimed Sandy. "Your ancestors made a promise."

"But that's the only way my dad can get the money to help my brother," Mary cried out.

"No, it isn't!" Sandy said.

"What do you mean?" questioned Mary.

"We've some wonderful news to tell you," continued Sandy.

"What is it?" Mary asked.

"We know a doctor that'll help!" exclaimed Sandy.

"But we don't have health insurance!" insisted Mary.

"This doctor will help without it!" added Beth.

"How can this be?" Mary answered in disbelief.

"Because this is the doctor who tried to save my mom, but since the cancer had been detected too late, there was little they could do for her. But we can hope now that there's still time for your brother," said Beth.

With urgency in her voice Mary replied, looking directly at each girl in turn, "Then Sandy and Beth, you've got to talk with my dad. Help me convince him that what he's doing is wrong!"

"We can talk to him now!" urged Sandy. "We'll just get on our bikes—"

"He'll be back the day after tomorrow. He went to tell his sister, who lives in the Upper Peninsula, about his decision to sell the family farm," said Mary distraughtly. "But if he doesn't listen to us, there is something I'm terribly worried about!" Mary added, and her body became rigid.

"What is it?" inquired Sandy.

"My great-grandmother's spirit. She must know that we're doing everything we can to make sure the developers aren't going to destroy her home. I'm really scared that if she thinks the bulldozers are coming, she'll evoke the curse on the entire Miller family! Maybe she'll even do it tonight! It's possible! I just don't know when she'll do it! We've got to let her know!" said Mary anxiously, her facial features tensed up like a rigid statue outlined in a bright red flush.

"But how?" inquired Sandy.

Mary lowered her eyes and her voice went down two octaves. "I'll speak to her tonight."

"Not alone. We'll go with you," insisted Sandy, and as she spoke these words, her stomach turned over.

"You're not afraid?" questioned Mary.

Sandy and Beth exchanged quick glances to one another and hid their fear when they turned to Mary and said, "No! Of course we're not."

"The only problem is sneaking out of my house at night for such a long time and not being noticed," said Mary.

"I've an idea!" Beth exclaimed. "Why don't we say the club is having a campout in my backyard, near the pond, and when my dad's asleep, we'll go to the haunted—I mean your great-grandmother's house."

"That's a great idea!" Sandy agreed.

"I don't think my mom will let me camp out," said Mary.

"Don't give her the chance to say no!" insisted Sandy. "Tell her if she says yes, you'll do extra chores for a month. *NO*, say a year! Anything to make her happy! Only be sure you're at Beth's tonight, around 7:00!"

CHAPTER 14

Haunted House

Sandy telephoned the other club sisters, but only Lynn's, Beth's, and Sandy's parents agreed to the campout, because the weather report predicted evening thunderstorms. The three girls had convinced their parents when Sandy thought of presenting weather facts to them. Her strategy went something like this: "Mom and Dad, did you know that the number of times that the weather reports are wrong is more than fifty percent?!! And why allow a predicted weather report—that is more than likely wrong—ruin the planned fun of ten twelve-year-old girls?" Only three sets of parents bought the logic. Since the Millers were phoneless, Sandy had to wait until evening to learn if Mary was permitted to join them.

In the meantime, a myriad of preparations were necessary, if the campout was to be successful. First and foremost was sequestering a tent. Obtaining this critical camping gear would be challenging. Sandy had to approach her brother, Frank, to borrow his new tent. Whereas Sandy usually knew how to obtain her needs from Linda with sweet talk, Frank wasn't as malleable. He had certain moral convictions—one, which dictated that his newly purchased items were for his use only. Sandy's solution? *Bribery! But with what?* she wondered.

Frank, at fifteen, was already the entrepreneur of the family. He was fortunate enough to have experienced several business successes with his creative ideas. For example, one year he said to his father, "Dad, no one is selling rock salt near your store, not even you. I'm convinced selling rock salt will be a gold mine! Dad, I'm willing to invest a thousand dollars of my Bar Mitzvah money, if you'll match it and let me sell it at the store after school, and on Saturdays."

You see, Frank noticed that customers, who wanted and needed rock salt to melt their snowy and icy driveways and sidewalks, had to travel out of their way to purchase it. Since Midwest winters often produced ice and snow for four to six months out of the year, and since customers needed and wanted the item, Mr. Lowenthal agreed to the plan. The rock salt sold like hot cakes, producing great profits for both Mr. Lowenthal's hardware business and Frank's wallet. Frank's only problem was the profits never seemed to be large enough, because as soon as he had extra cash, he would buy gadgets, large and small. He loved to purchase novelties. The flashier and more expensive the item was, the happier Frank seemed to be.

Sandy noticed that Frank, for the last several weeks, was buying beautiful, exotic fish for his aquarium. She observed that her brother enjoyed feeding his fish, but hated cleaning the aquarium. *That's it!* Sandy said to herself. *I'll get Frank to lend me his new tent, if I promise to clean out the aquarium, the next time it needs to be done.* With this brilliant idea, Sandy was now prepared to negotiate with her brother.

"No, way!" yelled Frank. "You're not borrowing my new tent!"

Sandy, anticipating this reaction, remained calm. "You're right, Frank. What a crazy idea, thinking I might be able to borrow your new tent. I mean you probably wouldn't have a second thought if it was already a year old."

"Not even if it was five years old!" shouted Frank.

Sandy, still composed, moved closer to the aquarium, observing the fish dart back and forth. Using Frank's tent was proving more difficult than Sandy had anticipated. *Now, I'm gonna have to go to battle!* She pulled her shoulders back, straightened her posture, and turned to face the enemy.

"Frank, this aquarium in your room is really great. I mean it's really beautiful! Not many teens have a fish tank like this—I mean look at all these unusual-looking fish. What's this one called?"

"That's a clown fish. It's really cool, isn't it," said Frank, sitting on his newly purchased leather reclining chair.

"Unbelievably cool, man."

"Tomorrow, I'm buying my most exotic fish yet, a Siamese sword-fighting fish!" Frank boasted.

"Wow!" exclaimed Sandy. "That'll make your fish tank look awesome!"

"You betcha!" Frank said, watching an angelfish dart across the tank.

"Frank, I noticed that every few weeks you clean out the entire aquarium. I see you taking your fish out and putting them in bowls with water. Then, scrubbing the inside of the tank to get off the algae and grime. That's a big job!" exclaimed Sandy.

"Yeah, it's a drag. It takes forever," Frank moaned.

"Especially when you'd rather be at the store, looking for a new exotic fish to buy," said Sandy.

"Wouldn't that be nice," sighed Frank, as he continued watching the chase.

"When's the next time you gotta clean it?" inquired Sandy.

"Well, the algae are already forming over here. But I probably could get by with another week," said Frank, as he folded his hands behind his head.

"Frank, I'm gonna give you the opportunity to be at the store, buying a fantastic tropical fish, the next time you need to clean this aquarium," said Sandy.

Finally taking his eyes away from his fish tank and looking straight at his little sister Frank said, "Oh, yeah? And who's gonna clean it? Mr. Clean?"

"Me! If you let your baby sister borrow your tent tonight."

"You really want to use my new tent, Sandy?" Frank asked, now busily adding more colored stones to the bottom of his aquarium.

"It'll help make the campout more fun."

"On one condition," said Frank.

"What's that?"

"If you clean the aquarium for the rest of the summer, you can use it tonight," Frank smirked.

"For the rest of the summer!" Sandy shrieked. "Now you've gotta be out of YOUR mind! I use the tent for one night and you want me to work all summer!" screamed Sandy.

"Take it or leave it. It's my one and final offer," insisted Frank, and he returned his attention back to his aquarium.

Frank was truly a tough negotiator. Sandy hadn't anticipated this tough a bargain. Sandy was in a bind. *In order to make our secret getaway, we gotta use Frank's tent.* Knowing Frank had the upper hand, she said, "Okay, Frank, you win this time."

"I knew you'd see it my way!" gloated Frank.

Later that evening, Sandy's dad dropped her over at Beth's house and helped her carry the large boxed tent into Beth's backyard, and placed it on the ground. Seeing Sandy, Lynn and Beth charged out of the house.

"Great, you brought the tent!" exclaimed Beth. Mr. Lowenthal told Sandy to have fun, kissed his daughter on the forehead, and departed.

"I practically had to give up my life to get my brother to let us borrow it!" quipped Sandy.

"You do know how to put it up?" Lynn asked, looking down at the box.

"How hard can putting up a tent be?" Sandy said. "Hey, we put together the award-winning volcano; we can put up a simple tent!"

"Oh, no! Beth, now we're in trouble. Sandy doesn't know how this thing works!" laughed Lynn.

"We'll see about that!" insisted Sandy, and she psychologically prepared herself for the challenge.

The girls spent the next ten minutes pulling the tight-fitting tent out of the box. That was easy. They then spent the next hour of a hot, humid, summer's evening trying to erect it. And not having much success. Sandy, with two tent poles in each hand, was sweating profusely. However, she was determined to complete the job. Every five minutes she swatted at mosquitoes and stopped to view the photograph of the erected tent on the box: positioned in a serene setting, next to a meandering river, against a backdrop of picturesque foothills.

"Oh, if it could be so easy," Sandy moaned to her friends.

Sandy hoped the photograph provided her with the critical clues, but no such luck. Then Lynn, looking at her watch, realized it was already 8:00 p.m. and wailed, "Mary isn't here yet. She was supposed to be here an hour ago! No tent, and no Mary—not exactly what we had planned! And not even a cool breeze," she added, with beads of sweat pouring from her brow.

"I don't mind the heat," said Beth. "It's these nasty mosquitoes I can't stand!" and frantically waved them away from her face.

"Don't worry. I'm sure Mary will come," Sandy said, "she knows how important this is." Using her hands to wipe the sweat from her forehead, Sandy went back to the empty tent box once more. This time she looked inside it. "*Voila!*" she proclaimed, pulling out the directions. "If at first you don't succeed, try, try again!"

Now with the coveted directions in hand, the club sisters figured out what they'd been doing wrong. Within twenty minutes, Frank's new green five-person tent stood by the banks of Sandy's all-time favorite pond in the world. The girls felt giddy about their success and were walking around their construction in awe, patting each other on the back.

Sandy shouted, "Come on, let's get our gear and go inside!"

The girls quickly collected their sleeping bags, flashlights and food rations lying on the grass, and rushed inside.

"This is really cool," said Lynn, plopping herself down into a supine position on her neatly rolled-out sleeping bag.

"I could learn to like living inside one of these on a regular basis," said Beth, stretched out on her sleeping bag, gazing out the screened doorway.

"Me, too," agreed Sandy, peering through the tent's small screened window.

As the girls marveled at both the tent's simplicity and functionality, Beth nervously glanced at her watch. "Oh my goodness, it's already 9:30 and Mary still isn't here!"

"Let's give her another hour, and even if she's not here then, we'll just go to the Haunted House ourselves," stated Sandy.

"Maybe she'll be able to sneak out of her house and we'll just wait for her there. Besides, we can't leave my backyard until we know for sure my dad is sleeping. And he never goes to bed before 11:00 p.m.," said Beth.

Knowing they had time before embarking upon their mission, they continued doing what twelve-year-old girls do best inside a tent—talk. The discussion was wide-ranged, from what were the coolest sneakers to buy, to Sandy's surprise at Lynn's revelation of her crush on Michael Levine.

"Well, now you know," replied Lynn, with her cheeks glowing.

"Are you going to do anything about it?" inquired Sandy teasingly.

"He has a baseball game next Thursday. I think I'll go and cheer him on," replied Lynn.

"That's a swell idea, Lynn. He's a nice boy and handsome," said Sandy.

"Yeah, I know," replied Lynn, with dreamy eyes. "What about you, Sandy? Don't you like someone?" inquired Lynn.

"I sorta like Freddy Cohen and I think he likes me," said Sandy shyly, which was completely out of character for her.

"Well, I know he likes you!" Lynn teased.

"And how do you know this?" Sandy persisted.

"Because he told me," Lynn smirked.

"And you never told me!" said Sandy, her green eyes stretched wide, as if connected to her eyebrows.

"Well, he just told me the other day when I ran into him, riding bikes down Tyler's Hill," insisted Lynn.

Beth didn't join the conversation. She hadn't even heard a word of what her friends said. She was clearly lost in her own thoughts.

Lynn and Sandy started giggling when Lynn was desperately and unsuccessfully trying to unscrew the water canteen's lid. Finally Lynn said to Sandy, "Here, see if you can do it. I'm really thirsty!"

"Sure," said Sandy, wiping her hands on her shorts. "Just shine your flashlight on it, so I can see better." Mustering all her strength, Sandy managed to do it.

Tyler's Hill

Lynn gratefully took a swig of water and offered some to Sandy. Getting back to their previous subject matter, she asked Sandy, "How old do you wanna' be before you get married?"

"Twenty-three or four. For sure, I want to wait until I'm finished with college."

"I want to marry and have four children," said Lynn.

"Wow! That's a big family, Lynn," said Sandy. "I just want two, a boy and a girl. That'll be enough for me."

Suddenly, Beth spoke, seeming quite disturbed. "What are we going to do without Mary?"

"First mistake. We should've had a plan if Mary couldn't come," said Sandy, perturbed with herself.

"But you don't have to," spoke Mary quietly, as she slipped inside the tent.

"Mary, you made it!" Beth sighed with relief.

"I just couldn't get here any faster. I was helping my mom with Timothy." Mary crawled next to Beth.

"Mary, I was getting so worried you weren't gonna make it!" said Beth.

"I almost didn't," replied Mary. "My mother almost changed her mind."

"We must go soon!" Beth urged, looking intently at Mary.

"I know," agreed Mary.

"No, you don't know," said Beth.

"Beth, you're talking so weird," said Sandy.

"I can't say anymore!" insisted Beth, and she peered out the tent's window. "Darn! My dad still hasn't turned off his light and it's 10:45! Mary, we must get to your great-grandmother's house soon! I mean really soon!"

"But Beth, it's just a quarter of the hour," said Sandy. "You told us your dad always goes to bed around 11:00."

"You don't understand!" snapped Beth. "We must get to the house before midnight!"

"But, why, Beth?" asked Sandy.

"I know what I'm talking about!" pressed Beth. "We must be there before midnight!"

The other girls glanced at each other with surprised looks on their faces, wondering about Beth's strange mood. Then, for the first time during the evening, the tent filled with an awkward silence, as Sandy, Lynn, and Mary sensed something was deeply disturbing Beth. The girls quietly lay back on their sleeping bags. The sounds of the crickets penetrated the tent's thin canvas. After five minutes, Beth turned to Sandy with an intense expression on her face.

"Sandy, didn't you ever wonder why I changed my mind and joined the club?"

"I just knew you would," answered Sandy, as she and the other girls sat up, curious to know the real reason.

"I know this sounds strange," she gulped, as she twirled her curls. "But . . . it was my mother."

"But, Beth . . . how can that be?" Sandy questioned. "You know that's impossible!"

"It isn't!" insisted Beth.

Sandy was trying to make sense of Beth's strange comments. "Now, I'm a little worried about you. I mean, Beth—"

"She came to me through my dreams. She told me to join."

The girls sat cross-legged on top of their sleeping bags looking wide-eyed, and Lynn and Sandy snatched quick glances at each other. They remained silent as Beth continued.

"Last night, she came again." Beth looked directly at Mary. "She said we must be at your great-grandmother's house before midnight." Mary nodded and seemed to understand. Sandy and Lynn were confused, but offered no rebuttal; they felt uncomfortable and shivers ran up their spines, but they didn't reveal their fear. They couldn't back out of the mission now. The club sisters were in on this all together.

Beth pointed her flashlight to look again at her wristwatch. It was exactly 11:00 p.m. She peeked her head out of the tent and then reported, "Coast still isn't clear. My dad's light is on." Beth and Mary sat quietly. Sandy and Lynn nervously waited, each imagining in one way or another whether they were really going to see a ghost tonight. Beth peered out again. "Yes! His light is off! We'll wait fifteen minutes, just to make sure my dad's asleep and doesn't hear us," insisted Beth. Waiting quietly for fifteen minutes inside the tent seemed like an eternity to the girls. But Beth knew if her dad didn't get up in the next fifteen minutes then he was sound asleep—allowing them to secretly carry on with the mission. Beth held her flashlight high above her wrist, allowing everyone to count down the minutes. All eyes fixed on Beth's watch, as if they were in a hypnotic state. They watched the large second hand move around and around. One minute passed, five minutes passed, ten minutes passed, and finally fifteen minutes passed! Anxiously, Beth peeked out again. This time she signaled, CLEAR!

Mary said, "Get your gear and follow me! I know the woods the best."

The night was still humid. Thick cloud cover hid the moon's light as the four girls slowly crept out of the tent into the blackness, like panthers slinking through the jungle. They strapped their backpacks on, and the beams of light coming from their handheld flashlights guided them to the lighted streets, where they quickly turned them off. Before leaving, they had arranged their sleeping bags and pillows to resemble them, as if they were sound asleep. This was a trick Sandy had seen in a movie once.

Cautiously, they proceeded to the Haunted House. In preparation for the mission, Sandy told her friends, "Now remember to wear black as camouflage. I know there is a curfew for kids our age, and we don't wanna risk being caught by the police!" So, every time a car passed, they were a bit nervous and tried to walk like cool, older teenagers. They swaggered their hips.

Mary whispered, "One more block and we'll be passing the subdivision—and we're in the woods!" The girls quickened their pace; their arms swayed back and forth. Sweat beaded up on their faces and poured down their backs, drenching their tee shirts. Sandy couldn't remember a more humid Midwest summer's evening. Finally, they escaped from the suburban streetlights and cars swooshing by into the blackness of the only remaining woods left in their community. Once in the woods, the girls experienced pitch-blackness and were frightened, until Sandy yelled, "Quick, put on your flashlights!"

"This is much better!" exclaimed Lynn, "I was tripping on the broken branches!"

"It's only a ten-minute walk to my great-grandmother's house," assured Mary. But as they slowly hiked through the dark woods, with only their small beams of light guiding them, it felt to Lynn, Sandy, and Beth as if it were taking an eternity to get there.

Nervously, Lynn crept up behind Sandy. "Sandy, how much longer?"

"Don't worry. We'll be there soon," whispered Sandy.

The girls continued their journey in silence until Mary burst out saying, "This way, down this path."

The girls carefully picked their way down the inclined path. Their eyes remained fixed on the small beams of light emitted from their flashlights. When they were brave enough to allow their eyes to sneak off the path, spooky shadows enveloped them. Before tonight, they never realized how dark and scary trees appear in the dead of night, in the middle of the woods, without even the benefit of the moon's light. Only a few stars blinked in the night sky.

Suddenly, Lynn screamed. "What wrong?" whispered Sandy, as she reeled around to look at Lynn's frightened face.

"There's someone behind that tree!" The girls held their breath and pointed their flashlights up and down and around the tree. Nothing appeared out of the ordinary.

"Lynn, it's just your nerves," Mary reassured Lynn, "it's nothing, probably just a squirrel looking for food. We'll be at the house shortly. And please, once we're inside, no talking! You must concentrate only on the appearance of my great-grandmother's spirit!" insisted Mary.

"Sure, Mary, whatever you say," said Lynn.

"Absolutely, Mary, you're in charge!" said Sandy.

"I'll be right by your side," said Beth.

After a few more minutes on foot, the girls stood directly in front of Miller's Haunted House. The few night stars cast an eerie glow around it. Mary, her flashlight illuminating the path, lead the girls directly onto the rickety porch, making it creak and quiver with their every step. Mary reached into her pocket and pulled out a key to unlock the front door. She entered, beckoning her friends to follow. Cautiously, Beth and Lynn entered the house. Lynn was telling herself to be calm. Sandy didn't enter the house immediately. She stood on the porch, noticing that suddenly the hot, humid, night air had drastically changed—a cool breeze swept out of nowhere, blowing her hair in all directions. She quickly turned on her heels and joined her friends.

In contrast to the cool breeze outside, the inside of the house was hot, and reeked from a terrible musty smell, for it hadn't been properly aired out in years. The girls' flashlights shone on the old wooden furniture from the 1800s that remained in the house.

"Okay, everybody. You must sit down and be quiet. Keep very still. And turn off your flashlights," said Mary, now clearly focused on the mission. When the girls sat down on the sofa, puffs of dust flew out. The girls remained true to their promise and said not one word. They watched their friend strike a match and light a candle positioned on a small round table. Its yellow glimmer revealed the old, tattered Bible Sandy had noticed when she peered into the house for the first time, last summer. The girls listened to Mary, attempting to conjure up the spirit of her great-grandmother. She was desperate to avoid the dreaded curse.

"Great-grandmother Miller, I've come here dozens of times to speak with you and you've never appeared, but you have revealed yourself to my father and my friend, Sandy. Now, Sandy is here with other friends, so that we can talk to you. We've something important to tell you." Mary took the burning candle from the table to guide her, as she walked about the small wooden house. Her shadow followed her, landing on the walls, distorting her image, and making her eerily appear five times larger.

Suddenly, thunder clamored outside and a minute later rain poured from the black skies, pounding the rooftop, making it difficult to hear Mary's voice. Sandy was grateful they made it out of the woods and into the house before the storm.

"Great-grandmother Miller, we've come to tell you that we won't let them destroy your home! I know that's what you're worried about," Mary declared.

As Mary continued, Sandy noticed the storm outside had dramatically worsened. The wind hollered bitterly, sneaking under the doorway and filling the room, making the candle flicker wildly. Hail pelted a window, shattering the glass, startling the girls, and stopping Mary's voice cold. Sandy rushed from the sofa, flung the door open and stepped onto the porch. What she saw terrified her. Her knowledge regarding tornadoes informed her that weather conditions were possible for a twister to develop. She tore back through the house.

"The weather is really getting bad!"

"Be quiet!" Mary responded angrily. "I told you earlier you can't talk! You're disturbing my great-grandmother's spirit!"

Sandy slunk back down next to Beth and Lynn who were clutching each other's hands, watching Mary, and not at all concerned about the brewing storm. However, Sandy's mind concentrated on the storm. She anxiously listened to it and thought about where they'd go if they had to flee. Quietly, she rose from the couch, flashlight in hand, and began walking about the house looking for a basement. Finding none, she recalled that old homes like this didn't have basements, but she remembered they often had cellars.

"Sandy, what are you doing?" Mary yelled angrily. "Sit down! You're making me lose my concentration. Can't you see you're disturbing us?"

"Okay. Okay! I'll sit down. But first tell me, does this house have a cellar?"

"Yes!" snapped Mary. "By the side of the house. Now, just be quiet!"

As Sandy returned to the sofa, Mary continued trying to conjure up the spirit, but to no avail. She was becoming frustrated. Suddenly, Sandy heard strange sounds. She again rushed outside. The earlier evening's thick cloud cover had disappeared, allowing the full moon's light to shine, revealing to Sandy that no more than one hundred yards ahead was a tornado! Running inside she shouted, "Everybody to the cellar! It's a twister! Mary, quick! Take us to the cellar!"

"Follow me!" yelled Mary, and quickly blew out the candle.

Beth, Lynn, Sandy, and Mary scurried outside, barely able to move from the porch, because the wind kept forcing them back. Terror seized the girls. Even with their eyes squinted half-closed to shield them from the blowing debris they, too, now saw the black, spiraling funnel-shaped twister, only fifty yards away—and coming straight at them! House debris blew everywhere. The porch tore off and was swept away, miraculously missing the girls. They feared for their lives. The tornado wailed like a siren, blaring out of control. The girls struggled to reach the cellar and used all their strength to open its shutter-like door. It didn't budge.

The girls started to panic and ran back to the house when Sandy screamed, "Come on back, we can do it! Our only chance is in the cellar! On the count of three, pull! Ready: one, two, three!"

Success! They scrambled into the cellar's blackness, sighing with relief. Huddled together, locked in each other arms, they trembled with fear, not knowing if they'd survive. The tornado's deafening sounds were coming closer and closer. Beth broke the hold to turn on her flashlight and look at her watch. It was one minute before midnight. She quickly shined the light up toward the ceiling of the small, cramped cellar, finding large cracks in the floorboards, allowing her to see inside the house. She yelled, "Look!"

Inside the house appeared an incandescent, white light, illuminating an image of a young woman. Mary shouted, "That's my great-grandmother!"

Suddenly, the image of a man appeared, his arms reaching out to the woman. The images lovingly and tenderly embraced. Then, just as suddenly, the light and the images vanished. There was complete silence. Lynn and Sandy were in disbelief of what they had just witnessed.

Mary whispered, "Finally, my great-grandmother is at peace with her beloved husband."

Beth nodded her head and embraced Mary, fully understanding the phenomenon.

Then, suddenly, there were sounds of glass shattering, right above the girls.

Sandy yelled, "We're in the eye of the tornado! Quick, grab onto the poles! Hold on tight!"

How long the girls stayed in this position, fearing for their lives, no one was certain. Then everything was perfectly still. The winds stopped howling; the whirling sounds halted—only the girls' rapid breathing was heard within the cellar walls.

"I think it's passed," Sandy announced hopefully.

The girls released their bear hug grip from the poles and climbed out from the safety of the cellar. They deeply inhaled the air's freshness, grateful to be alive and unharmed. An owl hooted in the distance. The moon's light revealed the destruction of Mary's great-grandmother's house. It lay in shambles, scattered everywhere. Only the cellar remained intact.

The evening's events were etched in their memories forever. Each was affected differently by the phenomenon. Lynn was in awe and completely humbled by it; for Beth it seemed to represent closure to the deep grieving process she had felt over the loss of her mother; for Mary—elation that her family could finally stop fearing the dreaded curse. However, for Sandy, the experience brought an unexplainable uneasiness and tenseness within her. She felt a surge of anger rush through her body, knowing that Mary's great-grandparents waited years and years to be finally reunited. What Sandy couldn't recognize was finally their spirits were at peace.

CHAPTER 15

A Gift

News of the tornado spread quickly, on both the radio and in local papers. However, this particular tornado was reported differently. Usually, television newsreels show the amount of destruction caused by a tornado. In this case, both local television and papers commented on not understanding how a tornado of such seeming fury created such little destruction.

The television anchorwoman reported, "Strangely enough, the only property destroyed was the old Miller house, built before the Civil War, located in Oak Park, Michigan. Not even the nearby trees were reported uprooted. Meteorologists and other scientists are baffled by the phenomenon, saying scientifically, this is impossible. They've never seen anything like this strange occurrence—a complete conundrum."

However, what seemed to baffle scientists didn't baffle Mary Miller and her club sister, Beth Fine. Having experienced the phenomenon, the girls were acutely aware that some occurrences are outside the realm of scientific facts or theories.

Two days after the tornado incident, Mary's father returned from his trip and Mary was anxious to tell him everything that had happened. "Sit down, Dad. I've some news."

"I know, Mary. I've heard about the tornado. It even made the news in the small town of Ramsey," replied Mr. Miller, with his face looking drawn.

"No, Dad, you only heard part of the story! Now, let me tell you the rest!" stated Mary.

Mr. Miller listened quietly at the kitchen table as a gentle breeze filtered in through the open window. Wide-eyed and sitting tall, his daughter shared the amazing story of how his grandparents' spirits finally were united, and at peace. When

Mary finished, she gazed deeply into her father's face. His worried expression, that she'd become so accustomed to over these last several weeks, had vanished. Mr. Miller felt a tremendous burden lifted from him now, knowing no curse lay over his family when the farm sold next week to the developers.

"Dad, there's something else we must talk about," said Mary nervously.

"And what's that, dear?"

"Are you still planning to sell the farm?" asked Mary, her hands gripping the sides of her chair.

"Of course, we still need the money."

"But, Dad, there's another way!"

"No, Mary."

"Dad, friends from my club know a good doctor. She uses the newest medical treatments, and she's willing to help!"

"But we've no insurance, Mary! Don't you understand?"

"Dad, this doctor will help without it!"

"No doctor today will—"

"Dad, this doctor will! You only need to bring Timothy in to see her this Friday!"

"Mary, is this really true?"

"Yes, Dad."

Mr. Miller was overwhelmed with this news. He stood and walked to the other side of the table and leaned down and embraced his daughter. He had dreaded having to sell the farm. Farming was the only occupation he knew. Knowing it was now possible to keep his farm and still obtain the medical attention his son needed was a precious gift. Mr. Miller, indeed, felt very blessed.

"Does your mother know about this?"

"I wanted to tell you first," said Mary, grinning from ear to ear.

Mr. Miller rushed upstairs to share the good news with his wife.

CHAPTER 16

More Ghosts

"Mom!" screamed Sandy, "look at this house, it's a mess! Beth will be here in a half hour!"

"I keep telling your father we need a bigger house. We've outgrown this one," Mrs. Lowenthal rebutted. "We could've bought one of the new homes, equipped with a modern kitchen and a family room. The homes are simply gorgeous! Only a mile from here, but, oh no, your father wouldn't budge! He has to be within walking distance to his synagogue!"

"Oh, so now it's Dad's fault that your religious magazines are all over the house, along with your used tissues, from all the creams you use?" said Sandy sarcastically. "No, it's *your* fault that this house is such a mess!"

"Knock, knock," Beth called, standing at the open screen door.

"Beth, you're early," said Sandy, clearly surprised by Beth's appearance, and feeling embarrassed that her friend overheard the fight.

"My sister drove me. It's so hot, I didn't feel like riding my bike."

"Well, come on in. I was just trying to get the house picked up," said Sandy with her face flushed red from anger. "It's usually not so messy, but—"

"Hey, we're Deep Talk friends now; you don't have to clean for me," declared Beth.

The girls walked into Sandy's bedroom and Sandy slammed the door. "You're right," said Sandy. "I shouldn't be picking up after my mother! It's her mess. You can't move an inch without finding one of her religious magazines, books, creams, or tissue boxes in the way! I mean, how can anybody live like—"

"Come on, let's just get to the game a little early," said Beth, trying to diffuse the tension.

"Okay, I just wanna' put on this new shirt," said Sandy, as she began to calm down.

"Oh, Freddy will like that purple top," said Beth admiringly. "Are you a little nervous?"

"I guess. It's the first game he's invited me to watch him play."

"It'll be such fun, Sandy. Come on, let's go!"

The girls strolled to Tyler School's baseball field under the glow of a warm summer's sun. Sandy saw Freddy warming up for his game. Freddy, from the corner of his eye, caught Sandy sitting down in the bleachers. He turned to wave. Sandy waved back with a big smile. She was really starting to like him. Sandy thought Freddy looked especially handsome in his baseball uniform, as she watched him run to catch a fly ball. The girls sat on the wooden bench under the powder blue, cloudless sky, and waited for the game to begin. Within five minutes, cars were filling the parking lot and more people joined them. Ken Dwight, a former classmate of Beth and Sandy's, also came to watch one of his buddies play. Seeing the girls, he approached them.

"Hi, Sandy and Beth. How's your summer going?"

"Fine," the girls answered.

"Hey, Sandy, your mother came to my house last week, trying to sell my mom one of those religious Jehovah's Witnesses magazines," said Ken, who seemed bothered by the incident.

"That's impossible!" barked Sandy.

"She said her name was Mrs. Lowenthal," protested Ken.

"You don't think there're other Mrs. Lowenthals in this neighborhood? And besides, my mother is Jewish. Why would she be knocking on people's doors, tying to convert them to become a Jehovah's Witness?" snapped Sandy.

"Sorry, I must have made a mistake," replied Ken. "I'm glad it wasn't your mom. Those people are really strange. They're constantly coming into our neighborhood and bothering everyone," said Ken.

Tyler's Hill

"Yeah, they bother me too," sighed Sandy. "Well, enjoy the game."

"I will." He charged off, joining his friends on the top bleacher.

As the girls watched the game, Sandy became unusually quiet. Beth realized that the conversation with Ken upset her more than she revealed. In fact, Beth noticed that ever since the tornado phenomenon, Sandy seemed easily agitated and irritated at the slightest provocation. It was even becoming difficult for Sandy to sit through the game. After the fourth inning, she jumped up.

"Come on, Beth, let's take a break."

The girls maneuvered down through the crowded bleachers, stepped onto the level grass, and ambled to Tyler's Hill, a short distance from the baseball field. Climbing to the top of the hill, they plopped down on its prickly grass. Sandy lay restlessly on her back, gazing up into the sky. Beth worried about her friend. Within a few minutes, Beth finally asked, "What's bugging you, Sandy?"

Sandy shot up and glanced at Beth with an icy stare. "Nothing!" she shouted and looked straight ahead.

"Ever since seeing great-grandmother Miller's ghost, you've been acting weird," said Beth.

"It's none of your damn business!" snarled Sandy.

"Oh, I see. Now, we're gonna start keeping secrets from each other?"

Sandy bit her lip, but remained silent. The truth was she had been feeling different since the encounter with Mary's great-grandmother's ghost, but was helpless to explain it. The encounter triggered muddled thoughts. More and more, she felt that her life was out of control. Sandy refocused her eyes and peered down into a nearby anthill. Hundreds of ants were climbing out. She watched. She watched as they marched toward a piece of discarded crust lying half a foot away from her. She watched as the "captain" appeared to order the phalanx to seize the food. She watched as the ants organized themselves to carry the long strip of crusted bread, weighing infinitely more than they did.

She watched as they paraded past her, carrying their prized possession down into the anthill.

"I hate her!" screamed Sandy.

"Who?" said Beth.

"My mother!"

"No, you don't."

"She embarrasses me all the time! Her going door to door, trying to change people's religions is driving me mad! I'm always lying to avoid telling the truth about her and her damn religion!"

"Then don't!" cried Beth.

"I can't tell people the truth about it!" screamed Beth.

"Why not?"

"I just can't! That's why."

"Then talk to your mom about it. Ask her not to do it so close to where you live," suggested Beth.

"Now, you must be crazy! My mom doesn't listen to anybody."

"But you still have a mom! You can try and work it out. Believe me, Sandy, you don't know how many times I wished I had my mom back for one minute, to tell her how sorry I am for some of the stupid things I did and said to her!"

"Beth, you don't understand! It's chaotic living in my house. You just don't know the half of it. You don't have to live with my mom!"

"But you do! You have to try and get along with her!" shouted Beth.

"No one in my family can get along with her!"

"You have to try, Sandy! I see how troubled you are by all this."

"Now you're a psychologist? You don't know what you're talking about!" shouted Sandy, as she tore down Tyler's Hill, abandoning Beth. She returned to the bleachers alone, but within a few minutes, she realized she wasn't in the mood to watch a baseball game and left.

CHAPTER 17

New Beginnings

Heavy. Sandy found it impossible to lift her head. This morning, as on each of the past six, since the twister phenomenon, Sandy's head didn't move from the pillow when she awoke. It felt weighted down, as though filled with lead. Linda had started a new summer job last week, so Sandy was alone in her room. Her eyes opened; she blankly stared at the white ceiling. The pink princess telephone rang. It rang three more times before Sandy dragged herself up, sat stiffly against the headboard, and reached for the phone.

"Hello," said Sandy weakly.

"Sandy, did you forget?" asked Lynn.

"Forget what?"

"Our weekly club meeting! Everyone's in my garage."

"I… guess… I did." She pulled the blanket up to her neck with her free hand.

"Just come on over. Get on your bike and just get here—fast!"

Sandy slowly got out of bed, went to the kitchen and poured herself a bowl of Cheerios with milk, ate only two spoonfuls, and pushed it away. She heard her mother downstairs in the basement and thought she was probably ironing.

"Sandy, is that you in the kitchen?"

"Yeah, it's me, Mom."

Mrs. Lowenthal was struggling to drag a suitcase upstairs.

"Can you give me a hand?"

"I'm eating my breakfast. Ask Frank."

"He went to the store with your father."

Reluctantly, Sandy went halfway down the basement steps to help.

"Sandy, dear, there are two more in the basement closet and they need to go to my bedroom."

"Why?"

"Did you forget?"

"I guess."

"I'm leaving tomorrow morning, for four days in New York, for the Jehovah's Witnesses Assembly! I'll be listening to G-d's word all day long, with thousands of other believers like me. Learning about the Truth. I'm so excited!"

Sandy only nodded her head and took the suitcases into her mother's room, then went to the bathroom to wash. When she finished, she dressed and went out to her bike, but she didn't head in the direction of Lynn's house for the club meeting.

She arrived ten minutes later at the wreckage sight of the tornado. Grey clouds passed overhead. It was the first time she'd been back since the phenomenon, a week ago. Sandy got off her bike and sat in the middle of the twister's debris, feeling as scattered as the pieces strewn all about her. There was no apparent reason for her to be here, but she was, and she was at a loss to explain it.

As she sat in the debris, she suddenly remembered the first time she saw Miller's Haunted House. She recollected climbing the old, rickety steps, peering through the windows and suddenly dropping the tadpole jar; running for her life, because she'd seen something move inside. Nonetheless, last summer, she knew for certain she didn't believe in ghosts. One summer later, she wasn't so sure. One week ago, she had encountered the most amazing phenomenon of her life, and she wished she hadn't. It caused her to think too much. She was happier one week ago, before the experience. Now, thinking about it all weighted her down.

She stared into the broken pieces of wood strewn about, wanting desperately to feel whole again. But who would help her? Tears washed down her face. Sandy finally managed to rise. She shuffled back through the wreckage and mounted her bike. When she dismounted, she found herself at the foot of Tyler's Hill. She lay her bike flat and summoned energy to climb to the top, where she remained, sullen, for the rest of the afternoon.

The next morning, Sandy's lead-head feeling still lingered. When she did finally rise, she heard commotion from the living room.

"Come on, Ruth, we've got to hurry!" said Pat Tanner, one of Mrs. Lowenthal's friends.

"Pat, will you stop rushing me? You know I'm not a morning person," pronounced Mrs. Lowenthal.

"Morning person or not, we've got a plane to catch in exactly ninety minutes! And it takes more than an hour to get to the airport. So, get a move on, Ruth!"

Mrs. Lowenthal was scrambling around the house in a frantic search. "I can't find my Bible! I can't leave without it, Pat!"

"For heaven's sake, Ruth, we don't have time to look for it now! You can buy three more at the Assembly."

"But it's the one that I've underlined all the important scriptures in," she said, as she anxiously checked an end table drawer. Finally, when it turned up under a towel in the bathroom, she smiled broadly and tucked it into her purse. "Pat, I found it! I'll just run and give Sandy a hug good-bye!"

"Hurry, Ruth, hurry!"

Mrs. Lowenthal knocked on Sandy's door. Sandy didn't budge from her bed. Mrs. Lowenthal knocked more loudly. "Sandy, I'm getting ready to leave for New York!" Sandy didn't answer. "Okay, dear, I'll see you when I return. I'll bring you a new Bible," her mother called through Sandy's locked door.

Sandy only forced herself out of bed when she heard the front door slam shut. She looked out the front window to see her mother pulling out of the driveway with her friend. Ginger, the family dog, sat up on her hind legs, her front paws on the window sill, also looking out, and barked as the car sped away. Sandy felt only relief that her mother had left on a four-day trip. *Four days. Four wonderful days without her!* Sandy thought. *I won't hear her fighting with Dad. I won't hear her Bible babble! And this junky-looking house will look nice for four straight days, because I'm gonna clean it, and my mom won't be able to mess it up with all her religious books, creams, and tissues all around!"*

Shortly after Sandy finished cleaning the house, the telephone rang.

"Sandy, where were you, yesterday?" questioned Lynn.

"I ... just ..." The words stuck in her mouth.

"I mean, Sandy, you should've been there. You're the club's president."

"I'm sorry."

"Well, you missed a swell time! My mom took all of us to the Oak Park pool. Next week will be our last meeting. We've got to think of something really fun to do. Come on over today, and we can figure something out. We've got to come up with something good!"

"Yeah, we'll figure something out. Listen, Lynn, I've gotta go. Ginger wants to go outside. I'll see ya later." She quickly hung up the phone.

But Sandy didn't see Lynn that day, or any of her other friends. Instead, she, again, found herself laboriously dragging her body, step by step to the top of Tyler's Hill, and slumping slowly into the grass. She stared out over the landscape and tried to clear the cobwebs tangled in her mind, but the threads held tautly. The only thoughts penetrating her brain were, *Four days, why couldn't it be four weeks, or four months, or four years that my mother stayed in New York, with her religious buddies?* And she found herself praying to G-d.

Please, dear G-d, make my mother stay in New York, so we can be happy. Make her stay in New York, so my father can have some peace. Please, dear G-d, please! Make this happen and I promise I'll never ask for anything else. I promise! And her eyes welled up with unexpected tears. She bit her lip and tried to hold them back, but couldn't. The taste of salt slipped into her mouth, as if it were being poured from a saltshaker. She remained on top of the hill for hours, and contemplated staying longer, but for the sudden and ferocious attack of mosquitoes.

Cloaked in a barrage of conflicting emotions, Sandy, drained of energy, walked down from her "mountain top," and headed home, where she wearily limped up the porch steps and entered her house. Mr. Lowenthal heard his daughter step into the hallway.

"Come on, Sandy, we're eating hot corned beef sandwiches and French fries for dinner."

Sandy, her bloodshot eyes making her look as though she were carrying the weight of the world, sat at the kitchen table next to Frank, who barely noticed his sister—he was too busy gobbling down his sandwich. However, Mr. Lowenthal noticed.

"Here, Sandy, dear, this will make you feel better."

Sandy took only a few bites and pushed it away.

"Hey, I'll eat that!" Frank said, "I'm starving!"

"You can't have it!" barked Sandy.

"Well, you don't seem to want it. And I'm still hungry!"

"I'll eat it later!" snapped Sandy.

"No you won't," Frank insisted.

"Yes, I will!" yelled Sandy.

"No you won't!"

"Yes, I will!"

"Children, children, that's enough!" Mr. Lowenthal said sternly.

"But, Dad, Sandy won't eat it. She's just being a stubborn brat!"

"I'm not! You're an idiot!" shouted Sandy and looking directly at her brother screamed, "You're the biggest idiot I know." She pushed her chair from the table and charged into her room, slamming the door.

A few hours later, when Mr. Lowenthal felt his daughter had likely calmed down, he knocked on her door.

"Sandy, it's me, Dad." Sandy didn't answer. "Please, Sandy, I want to talk with you." Reluctantly, Sandy opened the door. "Can I come in?" Mr. Lowenthal asked kindly.

"Sure, Dad." She climbed back up into her bed.

"Sandy, is there something you'd like to talk about?" He sat down on the edge of her bed. Sandy shook her head no. "All right then. I have a favor to ask you."

"What?"

"You know how we all help Baba walk to synagogue, due to her poor eyesight."

"Yeah."

"Well, it's your turn tomorrow."

"But, Dad, it isn't even the Sabbath tomorrow! Can't you get Frank or Linda? I really don't want to."

"They're both working tomorrow, and, besides, it's your turn to help your grandmother. At seventy-five, she needs us more than ever."

"But, Dad, I'd really rather not."

"And I understand that, dear, but sometimes whether we want to or not, it's a matter of responsibility. And it's your turn. I think you'll like going tomorrow."

"But, Dad, I don't like going to Baba's orthodox synagogue! Everything's in Hebrew."

"Not everything, Sandy, and tomorrow's a special day."

"What's so special about it?"

"Well, we've entered the month of Elul in the Jewish calendar. It commemorates the time in ancient Jewish history when Moses went back up on Mount Sinai for another forty days, to receive the second set of tablets."

"Wow, Dad, I didn't know he had to do that, but why?"

"Moses was seeking G-d's forgiveness, for his people's sin for praying to idols, when he left them the first time to get the Ten Commandments. When Moses saw this, in his anger, he broke the first set. Sandy, going to synagogue with Baba for this occasion is important."

"All right, Dad. I'll help Baba," said Sandy unenthusiastically.

"I knew I could count on you, dear," said Mr. Lowenthal, and he kissed his daughter on the forehead. "Good night, Sandy. I'll get you up at 7:30."

"So early?"

"All right, 7:45."

The next morning, Sandy halfheartedly put on a dress, and her father drove to her grandmother's house, which was only a few miles from their home. Sandy really adored her grandmother; she admired her kindness and devotion to the family.

And she loved her cooking, especially her homemade chicken noodle soup. Today, Baba was neatly dressed in a blue suit with her hair pulled back in a bun, covered by an attractive blue hat that complimented her soft, baby blue eyes. Sandy thought her Baba had the kindest face she'd ever seen. Even at age seventy-five, it was difficult to count more than two or three wrinkles lining the top of her forehead. She had a short stocky build, and plenty of energy, which allowed her to cook and clean for endless hours. Baba's refrigerator was always full—as if she could feed an army on an instance's notice. Baba—like Sandy's other relatives who'd come from Eastern Europe and learned English as an older adult—spoke with a thick accent. Her "w" sound came out like a "v" and "th" translated to a "dh" sound. Baba was peering out the window waiting for her granddaughter, and when Sandy entered the house, she lovingly embraced her.

"Beryla, you brought my Sandy!" And turning to Sandy she said, "My Kinder, you are lucky. Today, vhen ve are at synagogue, you'll hear the Shofar!"

"Mamalaben, I know you'll take good care of my Sandy," said Mr. Lowenthal, kissing his mother good-bye on the cheek, before he left to go to work.

As Sandy and her grandmother strolled arm in arm to the synagogue, only one city block from her grandmother's home, Sandy asked, "But Baba, today isn't the Jewish New Year, or Rosh Hashanah, or Yom Kippur, the Day of Atonement—why will I hear the Shofar in August?"

"Vell, my Kinder, let me see … how can I explain? Ah, I know! Your fadher tells me how vell you do in school. Vell, I bet vhen you take tests you study for dhem. Yes?"

"Yes, Baba, I always study for my tests. Sometimes a day or two ahead of schedule. I try and get all A's," stated Sandy.

"Vell, dhen, you'll understand vhy ve go to synagogue today—to spiritually prepare for dhe High Holiday of Rosh Hashanah, and Yom Kippur, a month from now in September."

Sandy and her grandmother entered the synagogue. It was a small sanctuary, decorated simply; a few stained-glass windows adorned the sides of the walls, with comfortably padded seats for the congregants. A half-wall called Mechitzah, in Hebrew, ran down the center aisle, dividing the space between, where the men and women prayed. At the center of the room was the bima, or stage area, where the decorative wooden ark was prominently located and contained the synagogue's most precious items—Torahs, the Jewish Bible. The Rabbi was standing on the bima, leading his congregation in prayer. Sandy sighed; it was going to be a long morning. She knew they'd be here for at least three hours, maybe four. She watched the men pray, with their prayer shawls wrapped about themselves, swaying back and forth, chanting in Hebrew. Finally, after about two hours of praying, Sandy saw the Rabbi come to the pulpit with papers in his hand. *Finally, it's time for the sermon*, she thought, which was always in English, the part she understood and liked the best.

"I begin my sermon this morning by us first hearing the Shofar."

Sandy saw a man with a long gray beard and covered in his prayer shawl, blow the Shofar—a loud penetrating, series of blasts. *If any congregant had fallen asleep, the Shofar blasts quickly woke them!* Sandy thought. The rabbi continued.

"We sound the Shofar today and every day during the month of Elul, except for the Sabbath, to wake us up, prepare us for our High Holy Days next month. We begin to reflect back over the year. What we did right. What we need to improve. What weaknesses exist in our character that need our attention? It's not for G-d to answer these questions. It's for each and every one of you. So, as the great fifteenth-century Rabbi Maimonides explains, we use 'the month before Rosh Hashanah, making our way back—to G-d, to our souls, to our true selves. As we get closer to the high holidays, we start looking back at our year and see that we've gone off the track here and there. We find that we have not allowed our souls to dictate our actions. The sound of Shofar is the wordless cry of the soul, yearning to break free of the prison of the mundane.'"

And of all the congregants sitting in the sanctuary, Sandy thought the Rabbi was looking at her when he made his final remarks of his sermon.

"Remember, G-d doesn't ask perfection from us, but the Almighty asks for us to be better, try a little harder, and to do a little more."

After services, Sandy walked back home to her Baba's house, where a feast awaited her. Her grandmother had prepared one of Sandy's favorite dishes: Hungarian goulash, a baked chicken cut into small pieces, and simmered in a spicy sauce and vegetables. Sandy seemed to have an appetite today and ate the meal hungrily. She spent the rest of the afternoon with her beloved grandmother. Baba told Sandy stories about the old country and she listened, wide-eyed, until her father came to pick her up after his work day.

Three days later, Mrs. Lowenthal, who returned from New York, was downstairs washing her dirty clothes from the trip. Sandy heard the telephone ring and ran to the kitchen to answer it. Eleanor, the neighbor down the street, was calling.

"Mom, the phone's for you," called Sandy.

Instead of running out of the house for the last planned club meeting, Sandy felt compelled to sit and listen to her mom's conversation.

"Anytime, Eleanor. You can come get the keys," said Mrs. Lowenthal, and she hung up the phone.

Within a few minutes, Eleanor was at their house and Mrs. Lowenthal handed her the car keys. As Sandy watched this interaction, she realized that people came to borrow items from her mother quite frequently.

"When do you need the car back?" inquired Eleanor, who seemed in a hurry.

"You could've used it all day, but I promised Mrs. Keller I'd take her shopping at three o'clock today."

"You're still taking her shopping, Ruth?" asked Eleanor.

"Well, since her husband passed last year, there's no one else," said Mrs. Lowenthal.

"Well, I wouldn't. She's such a nasty person," replied Eleanor. "And that dog of hers is always going onto other people's property!"

"She's just lonely," stated Mrs. Lowenthal. "And it's a neighborly thing to do."

"Well, I'll have your car back by 3:00," promised Eleanor.

She had seen her mother perform hundreds of acts of kindness to both family and friends in the past, but it was not until this moment that she saw her mother as a kind and generous person. She began to ask herself how many other positive characteristics had she also not seen in her mother, because whenever she was angry with her mother, which was most of the time, Sandy had always judged her mother.

Sandy realized she was already twenty minutes late to the last club meeting of the summer, so instead of riding her bike to Lynn's, she asked Eleanor, before she pulled away, if she could drop her off.

"Sure, Sandy, hop in."

As they drove, Sandy said, "You and my mom really seem to get along."

"Your mother is one of the kindest people I know. I don't know what I'd do without her as a friend and a good neighbor. I know she gets a bit longwinded with all her Bible talk, and she's doing her best to convert me, but I just ignore that." Eleanor finished her sentence exactly as they reached Lynn's house.

Sandy thanked her for the ride and darted to the club meeting that had begun a half hour earlier.

When Sandy arrived, everyone stopped talking and greeted her. Mary stood up and said, "I was waiting until Sandy got here before I shared this news." She took a big breath, and, beaming, announced, "My brother has been in treatment for the last several weeks, and at his last doctor's appointment, they felt he's going to pull through! Dr. Stone reported she hadn't anticipated seeing results this quickly, and felt she's been watching a miracle take place!"

The girls were deeply touched hearing this news, but none more than Beth, who quickly brushed away tears.

Mrs. Ernst entered the garage with a big basket under her arm, her eyes sparkling, and in her sing-song Jewish accent proudly stated, "I made my girls a surprise picnic lunch, since this is your last club meeting before school starts next week."

Lynn ran up to her mother and threw her arms about her neck. "Mom, this is wonderful!" Turning to her friends she continued, "Hey everyone, why don't we take this picnic basket and eat at Tyler School's playground, under the big shady oak tree?"

Everyone agreed, thinking it was a great idea.

"Come on, Mrs. Ernst, you come too," urged Sandy.

"Oh, no," chuckled Mrs. Ernst, "this is a special treat just for my girls. I know girl-talk these days is private. No parents allowed!"

Within the next five minutes, the girls mounted their bicycles and began pedaling to their planned destination. But not before designating Sandy as the person responsible for carrying the picnic basket, since she'd been given a ride to the meeting and didn't have her bicycle. Beth agreed to help Sandy carry the picnic basket, and the girls caught up to their other friends about fifteen minutes later. All the girls sat under the shade of the big oak tree chatting, some giggling over a "Knock-Knock" joke. And when Sandy put the basket down, Lynn started passing out the delicious sandwiches her mom had made, along with rugalas, a Jewish dessert—a semi-soft, crescent-shaped pastry sweetened with sugar, honey and nuts.

"Wow, rugalas!" Beth exclaimed. "They're my favorite!"

While they were eating, one of the boys' baseball teams was practicing. Lynn asked, "Do we see anybody we know?"

Sandy strained her eyes to see. "Only Ken Dwight, from our sixth grade class. Oh, and Lynn, I think that's Michael Levine, playing left field."

"Really?" said Lynn, and she immediately turned her head to look. Sure enough, it was the boy whom Lynn had a crush on.

Last week if Sandy had seen Ken Dwight, the boy to whom she'd fabricated the story about her mom not being a Jehovah's Witness, her stomach would've felt as if it were tied up in knots, but not today. She was actually feeling calm about it.

After the girls finished their picnic, some ventured off to play tether play. Lynn especially wanted to watch the baseball practice and Mary agreed to join her. Sandy and Beth climbed their favorite "mountain top." When they reached the top of Tyler's Hill, the view, although changed due to the plethora of new housing developments, was still serene and peaceful when one gazed to the north and west. Still, in these directions, green, open spaces and trees dotted the landscape. For many, including Sandy, the view from Tyler's Hill had a way of allowing people to see more than nature's physical beauty; it kindled their heart's inner vision.

"Beth, I've been thinking about the last conversation that we had up here," said Sandy softly, looking directly at her friend as they both sat cross-legged on the grass.

"About your mother?"

"I've not been fair to her," Sandy acknowledged. "Why, today is the first time I saw my mother differently."

"What do you mean?" questioned Beth.

"Well . . . today, I noticed she can be really kind and generous. And every time I hear her on the phone, she's always talking about one of her kids. How proud she is of us, how smart we are, and on and on. I mean it's really boring stuff, but that's what she tells her friends. I guess she really loves her children. And something else I noticed about her."

"What's that?" asked Beth.

"My mom's pretty."

"And where do you think you get your good looks from?" Beth pressed.

"Well, actually, I always thought that I looked like my dad."

"Not all of you, Sandy. You have your mom's eyes, mouth, and chin," said Beth.

"Yeah, I suppose I do. You know, Beth, I've not really given her much of a chance."

"What are you going to do about it?" questioned Beth.

"Well, the first thing I'm going do when we leave here is, I'm going to go over to Ken Dwight, playing baseball over there, and tell him that this is a free country! Meaning my mother has every right to go knocking on people's doors, telling them about her religion. Just like his mother has every right to tell my mother, if she chooses, she isn't interested in hearing about what my mother has to say!"

"Good for you, Sandy! But what's brought on this change?" questioned Beth.

"My grandmother's rabbi and you, Beth. You made me realize unless I work this stuff out with my mom, it'll be haunting me forever!"

"That's why we're soul mates," said Beth, and affectionately put her hand on her shoulder.

"But, Beth, something else is bothering me."

"What?"

"I know it's impossible for us to imagine now. But when we're old—like thirty or something, what if you get married, or move away from here?" Sandy said.

"Oh, that's never going to happen," Beth assured her.

"But it could. One day you may move away. Somehow we might lose track of one another! We'd be lost to each other forever!" stated Sandy.

"Now you're talking silly."

"Beth, it happens! Haven't you seen movies, where people have lost a relative, and they get private detectives to search for them? Sometimes they hopelessly search for years, never finding them!" exclaimed Sandy.

"Yeah, so," said Beth, not understanding Sandy's point.

"Well, if somehow we lose track of each other . . . "

"Don't be ridiculous," interrupted Beth, "that'll never happen to us."

"It's possible, Beth. It really, really could happen!"

"Well, then, simply hire one of those private detectives to find me," laughed Beth.

"Beth, be serious!"

"I am."

"Well, what if for some reason, I didn't have enough money to hire someone like that? I'd be going out of my mind! No, we must think of a plan," insisted Sandy, who seriously pondered the solution to the problem.

"Well, how are we going to find each other?" questioned Beth, who had now been convinced of the possible crisis.

"By staying connected to something we'll never forget."

Sandy, now pacing back and forth on top of Tyler's Hill, continued to contemplate the solution. She turned to Beth excitedly, and said, "I know! On your thirtieth birthday, June first, we'll meet right here, on Tyler's Hill!"

"That's a promise!" Beth exclaimed.

"No, Beth. It must be more. It must be a Deep Talk promise!"

Beth, who was still sitting on the grass, sprang up to face her friend to participate yet again in the sacred pact. The friends knew the routine; they stared deeply into each other's eyes while locking onto each other's outstretched arms. They again counted in unison and in a slow methodical tone boomed out, "One, two—Deep Talk," at exactly the same time.

Suddenly, Sandy broke the hold and started charging down the hill, like a torpedo in motion. Beth shouted after her, "For heaven's sake, where are you going in such a hurry?"

"To talk with Ken Dwight!" shouted back Sandy, her hair blowing in the wind.

THE END

LaVergne, TN USA
22 October 2009
161645LV00003B/8/P